In Stitches

True stories that

will keep you

In Stitches

by Edith Teasley

Cover design by Tommy Hardin

Longmeadow Publishing Company
Starkville, Mississippi
1997

This book is a book of facts. All names, characters, places and incidents are true. Any resemblance to actual events, locales, or persons, is entirely deliberate.

Printed in the United States of America.
1st printing; Sept. 1997

Library of Congress - Cataloging-in-publication data
Teasley, Edith, 1925 -
In Stitches / by Edith Teasley
P. CM
ISBN 09660655-0-6
1 - Short Stories
808.8   LCCN 97-91084

Dedicated to my four daughters
with more love than they can imagine.

Kay, Linda, Diane and Holly

Acknowledgments

My love and heartfelt thanks go to:

Linda, for acting as my critic, my sounding board, my best friend and my agent. For not allowing me to give up when I felt I had gotten in over my head, which was often.

Kay, who spent hours retyping my stories and compiling several into a booklet for the family.

Diane and Holly who encouraged me every step of the way.

Dr. and Mrs. Ed Lloyd for first suggesting that I write.

Assistant Professor Price Caldwell for his expertise and favorable comments that encouraged me to "keep on keeping on."

My friends at the Starkville Public Library for their gracious assistance in my search for information.

The Book Mart for their helpful suggestions.

Patty Archer at the Starkville Daily News.

Martha Ganss and Ed Grosinske for their interest and offers to help in any way they could.

Contents

A smile is rest for the weary,

daylight to the discouraged,

sunshine to the sad,

and an antidote for trouble . . .

Birdie, Birdie in the Sky

Santa Maria, California, is the land of golden hills, strawberries, horse farms, palm trees, beaches, sea gulls, warm days and cold nights. More importantly, it's the home of my oldest daughter and her family.

It is also the most perfect area in the world for growing broccoli, acres of broccoli that on a humid day can be smelled for miles. I am confident that the smell alone is the reason most humans cannot stand to eat it. The obnoxious green vegetable has such a strong odor that it can cling to your sinuses for weeks after leaving the area, and you pray that no one else can smell it. However, when you have family living there, as I do, you learn to accept that's the ONLY bad thing about Santa Maria when you miss them so much you just have to visit.

The wonderful things about the city are unlimited. I love the ocean—not in it, out of it. I love sitting on the beach, reclining under a huge umbrella, from the balcony of an ocean-front condominium, or walking out on the pier. I do occasionally walk at the edge of the water getting my feet wet, but well out of reach of the jelly fish, the sea weed, the undertow and many other things that we have never been told about. This way, I come home with all my body parts still intact.

During my last visit we decided to "do" San Francisco. We wanted to spend time at the beach, lunch at Fisherman's Wharf, ride the cable car, and walk through Chinatown. One of my granddaughters decided to take a day off and go with us. This was an added treat, since I am not with her as much as I would like. Now, this young lady is (and has always been) "full of herself." In fact, I expect that is the understatement of the year. The mouth goes non-stop. There is no need to worry about conversation because she talks constantly (to anyone, anywhere, about anything). I have never known her to be at a loss for words, nor has anyone been able to suggest perhaps someone else might like to say something. The family has simply learned to tune her out when the ears begin to hurt. The only thing I know that will make her quit talking is to ask her to sing. She sings like an angel, so that is a blessing. She is beautiful, smart, fun to be with and vivacious—always the center of attention, and loves being there.

Our day at the beach began really well. The gentle ocean swells were hypnotic to watch, the weather was perfect and the cries of the seagulls were like music to my ears as we walked out the seemingly endless pier.

My beautiful, irresistible granddaughter was running ahead of us, catching the attention of all the young men (and all the old men) and receiving envious looks from the females. I hope by now I have been able to convey a pretty good mental picture of her for you.

Seeing her suddenly stop and look upward, I was able to get her in the window of my new camera. She was a vision of beauty. . . her hair blowing in the wind, smiling and carefree. I got all of this on film. I also got a perfect picture of the moment a seagull bestowed a "deposit" that landed right in her face. For about thirty seconds she stood frozen, not moving a muscle, speechless for the first time in her life. Suddenly she took a deep breath, let out a scream and yelled, "Did you see what that bird just did to me?"

Now, I am the first to admit it was a terrible thing to have happen, and without a doubt it was a very rude thing for that seagull to do. But, her mother and I started laughing, and the harder she cried the more we laughed. We were hysterical. Bless her heart, my granddaughter was yelling for us to get "it" off her face, that "it" was hot, that "it" was sticky, that she could not stand "it," that she was going to die, and that she hated us. Well, the harder she yelled the harder we laughed. We could not have stopped laughing if our lives depended on it, and from the expression on her face I am sure we had just about reached that point. We were finally able to lead her to a restroom, and with the aid of wet paper towels we cleaned most of the bird "poop" off. I must admit that bird had to have been the size of a baby elephant from the size of the surprise gift it had dropped.

After Teresa calmed down enough to go out in public again, we headed home. The trip was very, very quiet. For the first time I saw my granddaughter at a loss for words. Of course, we knew it was simply the calm before the storm. So I tried telling her that it was the bird that had done the bad thing. She reminded me it wasn't the bird that kept laughing.

Common sense tells me she will get even some day, so I am a little reluctant to be alone with her. I have tried suggesting we need to put the entire incident behind us and get on with our lives. She smiles sweetly and replies, "In your dreams, Grandmother. In your dreams."

One Tomato, Two Tomato

Home grown tomatoes are one of my favorite foods. Big red juicy tomatoes, I really love them. Tomato sandwiches, served with a vegetable dinner, eaten by themselves, or in a crisp salad — any way you can imagine . . . I love them. Let me give you a bit of advice. The ones in the grocery stores with the little sticker that says "vine ripened", do not be fooled. That makes you think of home grown, doesn't it? That's exactly what the growers want you to think. They don't even taste like tomatoes. They may have been vine ripened, but they don't tell you where those vines were, do they? Probably in someone's basement.

Well, because of my love for the tomato, and because everyone else seems to grow their own, I decided I could grow mine too. That was a bad mistake on my part. Sort of like when I decided I would sew my children's clothes. They finally asked me not to try any more; they could gladly settle for fewer outfits if they could just get them ready made. But this is another story entirely.

Now, before I go any further, let me assure you I did not go into this venture blindly. I asked advise from friends, neighbors, strangers, and anyone who would listen. Obviously, from the luck I had I must have asked a few of my enemies.

First I was told I would need plenty of space in order not to crowd the plants. This was not a problem since I only had two plants anyway. Digging the area was not so simple. I quickly learned that what I thought was a normal, everyday yard was in reality a layer of concrete, hidden beneath a thin layer of dirt. I do not normally impose on my neighbors, but the importance of my project forced me to make an exception. A man that lives close by brought his tiller over to break up the ground. "Won't take but a couple of minutes with this little baby," was his remark as he assured me I would be able to start planting in just a very short time. Two hours later he started home without saying good-bye, and I did notice the tines of his tiller were all sitting at really strange angles. Surely it is my imagination that he is no longer as friendly as he once was . . .

Other "good" advice included purchasing barnyard fertilizer. Do you know what they mean by this term? I did not, and I still can't believe they use it to grow things we eat. Next, someone said Miracle Grow was an absolute necessity; still another said good rich soil mixed with organic humus (I didn't even ask what that was). Epson salts was given credit for wonderful tomatoes. I also needed a good water sprinkler that would ensure my plants would not go thirsty.

Last, but not least, I was warned about all the insects and all the diseases I might encounter. Naturally, there was not one spray that would take care of all the horrible things I had to guard against. The insecticide people are not stupid.

Then, as if the above mentioned items were not enough, I was reminded I had to have a wire cage to support each plant as it began to grow.

Armed with my list and my check book, I went straight to Wal-Mart Garden Center and purchased every item. Not only did I get it all, but being the smart shopper that I am, I purchased the large economy size. My ticket totaled $87.50. This included a book titled "The Joys of Gardening." Whoever wrote this literary gem should be placed in solitary confinement and forced to write another titled "I Lied About the Joys of Gardening."

Well, eventually my little plants began to grow. True, they grew very slowly, but I felt I could see some progress about every 10 days. I went out every day to pull the "suckers" that I had been told would stunt their growth, and one morning I discovered a tiny bloom. Can you imagine my joy? Just to think that one day that little thing would develop into a real live tomato.

Well, my joy was short lived. That was as far as anything went. No more growth, no more blooms, no more nothing. You know why? No one, and I mean no one, bothered to tell me I had to have lots of sun. I do have a little that filters through the limbs of the old pine trees in my back yard, but not the really hot, scorching, all-day sun needed to grow tomatoes. In fact, I thought it was pretty clever of me to plant where there was lots of shade. It would certainly have been more comfortable when weeding and picking the vegetables.

Well, noticing my deep depression, a really very dear friend offered to take my two plants, replant them in her garden, and nurse them back to health. She assured me they were doing well, but suggested I not try to visit them for at least three weeks.

In closing, I do not recommend gardening for the faint-hearted. It will deplete your bank account, play havoc with your nervous system, embarrass you in front of your friends, and strip you an of any shred of self-confidence you ever had. Bungee jumping would be easier.

Incidentally, if you know of anyone who needs fertilizer, Miracle Grow, a garden sprayer, two wire cages, and a large assortment of insecticides, I know where they can get a really good deal . . .

What A Way To Go!

So many of my friends worry endlessly about things that, to me, do not require any worry. I mean, if EVER we should be completely free from worry it must surely be when we leave this planet permanently. I certainly don't worry. I know what is going to happen, but I don't worry about it.

For example, my will. The only <u>will</u> I have to worry about is <u>will</u> anyone come to my funeral? The children and their families all stay so busy I can't imagine them having time to attend the services. I recently took a survey to see exactly when the best time would be for them. It seems the second Tuesday of each month after 10:30 p.m. would draw the biggest crowd.

The funeral home says this is a little late for them and I can understand their problem . . . I just can't find a solution for mine. I guess when I said I don't worry about anything I wasn't completely honest.

One son-in-law suggested I just forget any service altogether and go straight to my final resting place. Now, I have to admit this is another thing I worry about. I am really not satisfied with where the family plans to put me. I will be sort of packed in, because of lack of space, between two other family members. I am afraid they will have to force me in sideways. I can't sleep on my side, never have been able to and see no reason to start at this late date!

I don't mind that I will be sort of at the very edge of the cemetery, but I do hate to think I will be within spitting distance of the equipment shed.

Another thing, I have it on good authority that two plots down is the grave of one of the most notorious bootleggers from fifty years ago.

O.K., I know that was a long time back, but I can just see his old customers coming to pay their respects and sitting on my tombstone to talk about the good old days.

Another son-in-law suggests the family just put me out on the curb and let the city be responsible. Still another has offered to haul me off in the back of his pick up truck. There is nothing on earth as precious as a caring family!

What to do with my estate? The children have worked that out for me too. They plan to draw numbers to see who gets what, and then that person will have to be responsible for hauling the item to the dump.

My sofa is the biggest problem as it is the heaviest piece of furniture. As a dear friend of mine tactfully put it, I purchased it over sixteen years ago so naturally it is quite faded, but I love it. It's like a friend of the family. I could have it reupholstered, but it is so big it would be cheaper to buy a new one! Right! You know what would happen then don't you? I'd pass away and someone else would get my new sofa. Talk about hard feelings among the survivors! I say let everyone buy their own, pay a little down and a little each month like I did. It builds character.

Hot Tub Experience One Columnist Will Never Forget

I know I have mentioned many times that I have four wonderful daughters, but I am not sure if you know I have a brother and a sister. My brother is the oldest and he is the brain of the family. My sister is the youngest (six whole years younger as she is fond of saying) and although she is smart, too, she is extremely funny. I have always thought she probably could be a comedian. Instead, she chose to get married and raise a family.

Now, there is certainly nothing wrong with that. It just isn't very funny. Try finding humor in ironing a basket full of clothes, washing dishes, dragging a vacuum cleaner around from room to room, preparing three meals a day, and mopping or waxing the kitchen floor. Well, once in a while something comes up that makes up for the dullness of everyday living. For example, the trip we made to visit her daughter in Soddy Daisy, Tennessee. The name alone should have been a clue that we were in for a special time, not to mention the chance to be together and enjoy each other.

I've been told that Soddy Daisy has not always been a prime location to build a home, but let me assure you that has changed, at least in part of that area. It is now for the affluent. Restrictions galore are on everything from the color of your home to the care you give your lawn. If your taste offends anyone in the neighborhood, a "watch committee" calls on you and you are advised on the problem and given a certain length of time to correct the matter . . . or you can relocate.

Everything about the home impressed me — everything! The kitchen most of all. However, I am convinced there is another home somewhere that they really live in. This one is strictly for show. The cabinet under the sink must have been planned by an interior decorator. Even the items stored there looked as if they had been chosen for their color and shape and placed in a perfect spot in order to enhance another item.

Knowing that we had been traveling since early morning and that we were hot and tired, my niece asked if I would like to freshen up and relax in the hot tub before we ate. It sounded like a good idea to me, so I followed her upstairs to the master bedroom and through to the bath. Both rooms were testimony to her decorator's talent. However, by now I am a little tired of going on and on about how wonderful everything is. I mean, let's face it, I may not have a hot tub but I have hot running water and am darn proud of it. At any rate, she asked if I needed anything and I said no. She asked if I knew how to operate the tub and I said yes. Really now, how complicated can a tub be?

Everyone knows I am a senior citizen, and I feel as though most you are too, so you will understand what I am going to discuss next.

When older people travel we carry more luggage than others, not by choice, by necessity. It is necessary for us to carry at least one extra bag just for our medications: blood pressure, heart, arthritis, indigestion, Flex-All, corns, bunions, headaches, eye drops, and last but not least, the ever faithful Metamucil. (If you do not know what Metamucil is you are too young to be reading this article.) But I digress.

I decided to take my usual dose while I prepared for my bath. Discovering I had forgotten a spoon, and because I did not want to go back down stairs, I decided to use the lid of the container. I would shake into it what I perceived to be the correct amount of Metamucil. I could then pour this into the glass of water and stir with the end of my toothbrush. (I've heard that necessity is the mother of invention, but it is also the father of many mistakes.)

THEN I decided to start the water for my bath. I still don't know what I did wrong; I only know that when I pushed the switch, I saw more water than in the Hoover Dam. It shot everywhere; up to the ceiling, across the wall, down the shower stall door, and over the side of the tub. Desperately trying to turn the blasted water off and grab something to mop it up with, I knocked the lid filled with Metamucil off the counter onto the floor. Do you know what happens to that stuff when it gets wet? It looks like something you would expect to find floating in the Everglades Swamp— thick, slick and ugly. The longer it sits the uglier it becomes.

Now, can you imagine what it looked like on that marble floor? I couldn't use one of the beautiful towels, but I needed something that would help me hide the evidence. I couldn't yell down stairs without confessing what I had done. First of all, Metamucil is very much an old person's remedy, and why should I let everyone know I am an old person. Secondly, it would be admitting I did not know how to use the hot tub. At any rate, I did what any clear-thinking person would do. I grabbed the sweatshirt I had taken off and started mopping. This was not an easy task; in fact, it was practically impossible. I wiped and wiped, and then I wiped some more. I wiped for what seemed like an eternity.

My sister called up stairs to see if I was OK, and I answered that I was still relaxing in the wonderful hot tub. Finally, they called that they were going on to bed in about 30 minutes. Well, I still had about three square feet of floor to get mopped up, but I felt confident I would finish in that length of time. Finally, when I was sure the floor was as clean as it had ever been, I rinsed out the shirt and hid it in my travel bag . . . still wet.

Now I worry a lot, and I am good at it. When I got in bed I started worrying about that shirt starting to sour, about what if my sister asked again what took me so long, and what if the floor wasn't really clean? Then I worried about how much I was worrying. Finally, I fell asleep but dreamed of trying to swim out of a pool of (you guessed it) thick Metamucil.

The next thing I knew it was morning, and while we were eating breakfast my niece asked what I thought of the hot tub. I'm sure that since I spent close to two hours in it she must have thought I found it pretty spectacular. I smiled as sweetly as I could and said (rather cleverly) that it was an experience I would never forget.

Practically as soon as I got home a letter came from my niece apologizing for the bathroom floor being so sticky. She went on about how embarrassed she was, and what kind of housekeeper I must think she was. Naturally, I answered her immediately, assuring her she was an immaculate housekeeper, a wonderful hostess, that the visit had been very special, and that I had not even noticed the floor . . .

Cars and the Gender Gap

Nothing can ruin my day quicker than knowing something is wrong with my car. I drive an '87 Dodge that has been a good loyal friend, like a member of my family. I know all of its peculiar sounds, every squeak, how the air-conditioner sounds running on high, etc. Naturally, I am very much aware of anything out of the ordinary. The trouble always starts when I try to explain things to the man who keeps my car running. I always drive in confident there won't be a problem communicating with him THIS time.

I think I have a problem with my car.
"What kind of problem?"
I don't know. I thought you could tell me.
"What is the car doing?"
Nothing right now. It isn't running.
"When it IS running, what does it do?"
It makes a noise.
"What kind of noise?"
A funny noise.
"Well, I can't hear anything now."
It isn't doing it now.
"When does it do it?"
Off and on.
"What does it sound like?"
It sounds like something is wrong.

Now his neck is turning a tomato red, and he seems to be gritting his teeth.

"Is it a grinding or bumping sound?"
That's right.
"What's right?"
It's a grinding or bumping sound.

This car that I have loved and cared for over the years just sits there, not making a sound and purring like a kitten, leaving me looking like a complete idiot.

"Mrs Teasley, I can't tell what is wrong if I can't hear the noise."
Can't you just check everything until you find it?
"Yes, ma'am, but you will have to leave it with us today."
I can't do that. I have a hundred things to do today.
"Then you will need to bring it back on a day when you CAN leave it."
I'm afraid to drive it until you fix it.
"I can't fix it until I know what to fix."
How much is it going to cost?
"I can't tell you that until I know what is wrong."
If I leave it with you, please don't get finger prints on the hood.
"I have to open the hood to check things out."
Don't you have any gloves you can wear?
"Mrs. Teasley, you might like to try the service shop just down the road."
I did, they sent me to you.

Precious Moments
Are Remembered Forever

Part I - The Trip

Everyone knows I am not a formal person. Wearing socks with my Keds is about as formal as I want to be.

However, I have always felt I could be quite formal should an occasion arise that demanded it. Such was the case when my nephew married recently. The beautiful invitation arrived with RSVP duly noted on the bottom, plus the enclosure card telling about the reception.

Everyone in the family received an invitation. This was their first big mistake. You just don't invite all of us to anything without courting disaster. "All of us" includes fourteen people plus Noodles, the cat, and Who Dat, the dog.

The wedding was to be held at The Whitlock Inn, a beautifully restored Victorian mansion in Marietta, Georgia. We made reservations in Atlanta since some of our group hoped to visit Six Flags while there. Marietta was about thirty to forty minutes away.

Everything got off to a smooth start as we rolled down the driveway — the van and two cars — and headed toward Atlanta. It wasn't until we were almost to Tuscaloosa, Alabama, that we discovered my youngest granddaughter had smuggled Noodles into the van in a travel bag.

We had to stop and get the cat food and kitty litter and then pray we could get her past the desk clerk in the hotel. Determined to make the best of the situation, and to prevent my daughter from doing bodily harm to the child responsible, the two of us waited in the van until rooms had been assigned and the elevator was waiting to take us up.

Our rooms were lovely, and since I was tired, I decided to relax in my room with Noodles when the others went for a swim. She was perched on one of the beds daintily licking her paws when one of the children dashed in to find her beach towel. The moment that door was opened, Noodles made a dash out of the room and disappeared.

My granddaughter followed crying and sobbing, "Noodles, Noodles, I want Noodles." Another hotel guest in the hall said, "Bless her little heart, she must be starving."

The cat was finally discovered hiding behind a huge potted plant and was taken immediately back to the room where she curled up on one of the pillows and looked at us as though she could not imagine what all the fuss had been about. I, on the other hand, was a nervous wreck. I fully expected the authorities to knock on the door and yell, "Police. Open up." My daughter said I watch too much TV. I replied that I wished I was home watching it instead of chasing a crazy cat down the hall of a hotel. Never being at a loss for words, she smiled sweetly and said perhaps they could arrange that the next time the family took a trip. . . .

Finally, it was time to load up the van and cars and head for the wedding. Several little things happened to sort of take the excitement out of the trip. For instance, my feet were killing me. My other daughter said I could not wear my Keds to the wedding. I said I had gone to the expense of having them dyed to match my dress, but she had threatened to put kitty litter in them and give them to Noodles. What really scared me was that I knew she would do it.

On top of that, we got lost. My brother had given detailed instructions to my son-in-law. We THOUGHT he understood them. He SAID he understood them. Marietta was only thirty or forty minutes away. We had already driven oven an hour and a half when we suspected something was wrong. The car behind us pulled up beside ours and another son-in-law, gesturing wildly out of his window, yelled we had passed our exit thirty minutes ago. The third car was trying desperately to find out what was wrong. Can you get a mental picture of this scenario? We must have looked like the Beverly Hillbillies. All that was lacking was a chair tied on top of the van with me in it.

After we back-tracked and found a gas station to ask for more instructions, we finally reached The Whitlock Inn — extremely late.

Part II - The Ceremony

Cars belonging to the wedding guests were being parked by attendants in the parking lot of a bank next to the inn. The two were separated by a brick wall that had about a three foot drop on the side of the inn. In order to save precious time, we decided to go over the wall, rather than go to the front and then back again, to reach the garden where the wedding would soon begin. Since we heard no music we knew the ceremony had not yet started. We assumed they had delayed the beginning to allow us time to arrive. NOT!!!

Now, no one had a problem with the wall . . . except me. My feet were killing me, my knees don't work as well as they used to (actually, nothing works like it used to) and I am an old lady. As I tried to crawl down the far side of this wall, my heel caught in the hem of my dress. It tore the hem out, of course, and pulled the seam at the waist loose. I tried to hide the damage by holding my right arm in front of the waist, and with the left hand I was holding the skirt up, hoping it would look as if I was trying to prevent getting the hem of my tea length dress soiled, you know, like Scarlet O'Hara. Instead I looked like Quasimodo in "The Hunchback of Notre Dame."

A hostess sort of floated over to us and said the wedding had just begun, and that if we slipped through the hedge we could find our seats without ever being noticed. I will always wonder why she told us that. We had never done anything to her. What she did not tell us was that once we were on the other side of the hedge we would be eye-ball to eye-ball with about two hundred other guests; that the ceremony not only was well under way, but practically over; and that the only seats left were about twenty rows back. I would have preferred to just go to the reception. I would have preferred to drop dead, but with her gentle coaching we pushed our way through the hedge. There was not a guest there who did not know fourteen idiots were disrupting the wedding. Not a soul looked in our direction, as though they thought by ignoring us we would simply disappear. Just as we found our seats and got settled we heard the minister say, "I now pronounce you man and wife."

As soon as the photographers began taking pictures, the guests were directed toward the front of the Inn once again. I noticed my family had "circled the wagons" so to speak. In other words, I was surrounded . . . as though to prevent me from any more embarrassing mishaps. It probably would have worked too . . . if I could have just skipped the reception.

Part III - The Reception

Still clutching my dress around me in hopes of hiding the damage done climbing over the three foot wall, I hobbled up the front steps of a huge front porch. Festooned with ferns, ivy and an assortment of live flowers, this beautiful old porch was host to a champagne fountain and sculptured ice.

I decided that I should mingle with the guests. I decided this all on my own. I wanted to let them know my nephew came from refined, cultured and gracious people. However, I knew I needed to do something about my dress. I turned and asked a lady if she had a couple of safety pins I could borrow. Now, I thought everyone knew what safety pins were. Obviously she did not. She just looked at me as though she had not heard me correctly, and then disappeared.

No matter . . . it was time for the groom to dance with his bride. This is the boy who could not walk until he was in high school; however, he had no problem dancing. The two of them were just beautiful. Fred Astaire and Ginger Rogers could not have been more graceful.

I noticed many of the guests had plates filled with food, so I (once again on my own) decided to check the cuisine out myself. I cannot begin to tell you the amount of food being presented. One reason is because I could not see. Candles are romantic and beautiful but you cannot see doodley squat with them. Candles were the only source of light. I turned once again to a lady standing by me and asked if she could see any catfish and hushpuppies. Suddenly she had some sort of seizure because she could not seem to be able to breathe and she, too, disappeared.

Well, I certainly was not going to make a fool of myself by selecting something I couldn't eat, so I walked over to where my nephew was going to toast his bride. This is the boy who would hide under the table if anyone tried to talk to him until he was ten years old. He certainly had no problem with the toast. It was beautifully done, and the two of them looked at each other as if they were the only ones on earth, and hoped it stayed that way. It was so tender, and so sweet, it made me start to cry. I was tempted to ask someone by me for a Kleenex. I changed my mind though; I didn't want to be held responsible for a third guest disappearing.

Extreme Public Humiliation

My daughter and her family that live in California planned a weekend shopping trip to one of the newest and biggest malls close by. It was to be an all day event, so Kay, my daughter, wanted to be both comfortable and well dressed for the occasion. They started early in order to avoid the heavy traffic between their house and Los Angeles. This particular stretch of the freeway is awesome and beautiful, but the way the natives drive will add years to your life. When I am in the car, I always close my eyes. You don't see very much, but then I figure what I don't know won't hurt me.

Reaching their destination, the first order of business was a visit to the rest rooms. With that taken care of they were ready to cruise the mall from one end to the other.

Noticing people looking back at my daughter and her husband, and that they were smiling at them, she felt even better about her choice of clothes. Women can always tell when other women admire them. Intuition I guess you call it. Her husband also remarked for about the third time that he thought she looked especially nice. Her steps became lighter, she held her head higher, shoulders were back and she felt almost radiant. Life was really good.

As they walked from one end of the mall to the other, they were still aware of the smiles and admiring glances from other shoppers. When they took the glass elevator to the second level, they noticed people below still watching and smiling. It was a wonderful day to be alive . . . so many smiling faces.

After a leisurely lunch on the mezzanine, followed by more shopping, they decided to make their last stop a jewelry store. Leaning over on the glass display counter to admire the diamond rings, they were oblivious to the crowd around them until they heard more laughter. To no one in particular, Kay remarked that she wondered if it was always so much fun to shop in the mall. Overhearing Kay, a sales clerk whispered in her ear, "No ma'am, but then we don't often have someone with the back of her dress caught up in her panty hose either."

Kay doesn't remember how fast they left the store. She doesn't remember much about the trip home. What she does remember, and never ever forgets, is to check her clothes carefully when leaving the ladies room. Very, very carefully . . .

There is One Good Thing
About Growing Old

Isn't it amazing that we no longer have to solve our own problems? There are experts on every conceivable dilemma we might find ourselves faced with. You have already guessed it . . . I have a problem, I need help!

Briefly, Santa gave my daughter a camcorder for Christmas. Her idea of fun was to get everyone on film as they came in the door Christmas morning at about 5:30 a.m. in our bathrobes . . . (this is the same daughter who claims to love me dearly) no make-up and hair standing at attention.

Do you get the picture? So did she, and she has shown it to family, friends and neighbors over and over again. The first time I saw this horror video, I went immediately into shock followed by deep depression which I am still trying to overcome!

I've always known I was no raving beauty, but I had no idea things had gotten so bad. I knew I needed professional help. I knew I was aging to some degree, but it seems I went from being "more mature" to being a really old lady fast.

It happens to all of us. It is the easiest thing on earth to do. You just breathe in and out on a regular basis day after day, and then suddenly you are an old person.

I made an appointment with a doctor no older than my granddaughter. Heavens to Betsy! I still have to tell her to keep her feet off the furniture and not to talk with her mouth full.

However, as I have said, I had to have help, so I decided to act like he was a real doctor. I told him I wanted to know if it would be possible to grow young again? He asked if I followed a proper diet, and I explained that I ate everything insight, so as not to miss any of the major food groups. He did not seem amused!

Exercise? Of course I exercise. Who does he think goes out to get the paper 365 days a year? Not only that, but I purchased an expensive exercise bike. Best investment I've ever made. It keeps the grandchildren occupied for hours, and it's perfect for hanging clothes on when ironing.

Then too, I walk many steps from the recliner to the refrigerator and back again. This is not some casual walk. I take brisk steps, head up, shoulders back, and long strides. He can forget the exercise bit. I have it under control.

"Now, what about your mental attitude?" he continued. "This can affect your emotions, thus affecting how old your perceive yourself to be."

I told him my mental state had been severely damaged when I recently stood sideways in front of the mirror and attempted to hold my stomach in. All that happened was I pulled a muscle in my back and haven't been able to walk normally since!

The last time I went shopping for my granddaughter, I simply asked the sales lady to show me something in a size seven. She could have just said she didn't think that was my size. It certainly wasn't necessary for her to faint and cause a disturbance.

I shared all of these things with this very young man in a white coat with credentials framed on the wall of his office. Do you think he understood? He did not. He stood up in the middle of my story about the lady fainting, shook his head as though trying to clear his mind, mumbled something about how he knew he should have gone into another line of work, and suggested I try another doctor.

There is one good thing about growing old. I'll let you know when I think what it is . . .

It's Easier Being Sick
If Your Doctor Is Good Looking

Part I

I have been blessed with more than I can say grace over. Four wonderful daughters, each one special, beautiful, tolerant of my shortcomings, thoughtful, caring and above all, they are dedicated Christians. I have good friends, my home, my church and until recently I have had reasonably good health.

Now, because I have spent considerable time in three different clinics, I am also blessed with three fine-looking doctors. I assure you I am not a shallow person. I have sense enough to know that good looks do not make good doctors.

I also know, however, it certainly makes the healing process much easier, plus it can help you keep your cool under some very trying circumstances. For example . . .

Let's discuss the reading material we find in the waiting rooms. The magazines are there to help us pass the time, right? Wrong! They are there to lull us into a state of semi-consciousness from sheer boredom, thus we are slightly tranquilized and easier to deal with once we see the doctor. Recently, I picked up a magazine in the office with headlines, "Roosevelt To Run For Third Term." Now I liked Roosevelt; I even admired Eleanor. She didn't have much going for her in the looks department, but she had an overdose of brains to compensate. At any rate, that era is over and done with. I say, let's put it behind us and move on. This is not an original statement. If you will notice, every politician that has ever been caught in a "boo-boo" uses the same phrase.

Next Problem: I resent having to weigh every time I go in the office. They all seem like intelligent people; can't they understand I am unable to lose weight? I've weighed the same since I was ten years old.

I was born needing a 6X diaper that had to be special ordered for a newborn. By the time they came I had already gone up another size. Once I forgot to pick up my next appointment card, turned right around, went back in and the nurse wanted to weigh me again. I didn't get upset and complain. Who wants to upset an excellent physician — especially if he is a good-looking excellent physician?

My final problem. I talk a lot when I am with my doctor. I know I'm not going to be in there long and I want to be sure I don't forget anything he might need to know. He listens to my heart a lot. At least, he would if I could quit talking. Once he put the stethoscope down, gave a huge sigh and said if he was going to listen, then I needed to quit talking, and if I insisted on talking then he needed to quit trying to listen. Well, heavens to Betsy . . . that was plain enough and I got the point. Was I offended? Of course not! If he was an ugly man I might have been, but he is not an ugly man. So I smiled as sweetly as an old lady can smile and simply waited until he finished listening to my heart, then I picked up the conversation where I had left off. I thought he only had a problem hearing when the stethoscope was in his ears. Obviously this is not true. It must have some residual effect since he walked out and closed the door while I was still talking. I'll need to remember to talk louder next time . . .

It's Easier Being Sick . . .

Part II

This article is dedicated to my number two doctor. Number two is not indicative of importance. It is simply the numerical order in which

I met them..

This waiting room had an aura about it that told me immediately I was being judged. Only a very few minutes were necessary for me to understand what qualified you as either significant, average, or just mediocre . . . not to the staff, to other patients. For instance, as I took my seat next to an elderly woman, she looked me over carefully, peered over her glasses, and whispered in a confidential manner that the man across from us had been waiting for over thirty minutes. She felt positive he was a hypochondriac. Then a lady walked out of the office and another woman gave a knowing glance and said, "She got called in almost immediately, and was back there for over forty minutes with the doctor." I started to perspire. What if I had to wait a very long time, and then was only with him for a few seconds? How would I ever overcome the humiliation? I decided that no matter how brief my consultation was, I would leave by the back door. I did not intend to tolerate hostile looks from anyone.

The next problem is a little embarrassing to discuss, and I hope no one is offended but the matter needs to be addressed. You know the little plastic cups they hand you when you are having a physical? REALLY! They may be fine for men, but for women it's strictly a hit or miss situation. Surely the medical profession can improve on this if they can perfect heart transplants, reconnect fingers that have been severed, etc. I don't think I am asking a lot, but women of America, we need to speak out.

This particular visit to this particular doctor was necessary in order to get an injection in my shoulder. This happy experience had been put off several times, having been warned about the pain involved by a good friend that obviously had an ugly doctor. When my doc looked down at me from his six foot four inches, smiled and said, "This isn't going to hurt," it DID NOT HURT. Actually, he could have given me several injections in both shoulders if he want to . . . just to practice. Besides, the thought crossed my mind that it would have been a very clever way to spend more time with him. Heavens to Betsy, just think of the envious stares I would have been given as I walked out the FRONT door with my head held high. The others still waiting to be seen would probably have voted me "Patient of the Year!"

It's Easier Being Sick . . .

Part III

Having been advised that I needed to spend some quality time with a specialist in Birmingham, Alabama, I started looking forward to a short, pleasant vacation. That's what it was like the last time I entered U.A.B. for a few days. Remembering how well the doctor and I communicated, and how wonderful the hospital had been, I was not dreading another visit . . . not exactly.

First, let me elaborate on U.A.B. As far as I'm concerned, it has put us on the map. I've always resented the way the rest of the world feels about the South. Admittedly, we are "low-man on the totem pole" in many categories, but we are not the slow-witted, backward, uneducated persons some folks perceive us to be. I especially hate the way they try to mimic our southern accent. It's as though we always have a mouthful of mush, eyebrows raised, eyelids half closed, and dragging our words out like an antique Victrola that needs winding.

Think I'm exaggerating? Listen to "In The Heat Of The Night" just for two minutes. What I am trying to convey here is that we have MUCH to be proud of in the South and U.A.B. is right at the top of the list. Makes me want to stand on top of a tall building and shout to the rest of the world, "We have something you don't have. We have U.A.B."

Previously, my room was in the Pavilion, a section of the hospital designed to make patients feel good while they are feeling bad . . . it works. Beautifully decorated spacious rooms resemble a luxurious hotel, and because this wing offers more privacy than usual, it attracts celebrities.

Needless to say, I was pleased to know they had a room available for me, so with my flannel gown, fuzzy Donald Duck slippers, and a large Kroger sack holding my personal belongings, I was wheeled into my room.

I even wore a pair of very large, and very dark sunglasses that belonged to my granddaughter, hoping everyone would think I was a famous person attempting to arrive incognito. My daughters said I looked like a homeless person who had wandered in off the street. So much for looking famous.

Knowing in advance that I was going to be in Birmingham to discuss having a pacemaker installed, I had already spent considerable time practicing exactly how I was going to tell the doctor I had decided I did not want this extra piece of equipment attached to my body permanently. It had worked before, I saw no reason why it would not work again. This was before he reminded me who was the doctor and who was the patient. Then he explained why I did not have a choice, and he explained it in terms that even I could understand.

After this conversation, I was more than ready. He made me see the light. Whatever he thought was best. How soon could we get started? Did he think one would be enough??

I was anxious to please this man who was going to cut a hole in my chest. After having been given a shot of something that made me feel really wonderful — but made my tongue three times it's normal size — this same fantastic doctor took the time from his busy schedule to push my stretcher down the hall, into the elevator, and onto the floor where they prepare you for surgery.

I wanted to thank him for being so good to me, but the words came out, "Ah, thin dis ith weally wice ob oo." He just grinned and said it was part of his job. Looking back now, it <u>could</u> have been an orderly that pushed the stretcher — it <u>could</u> have been an orderly that operated on me, and guess what . . . I could <u>not</u> have cared less.

It's Easier Being Sick . . .

Part IV

Still feeling the effects of that marvelous shot I mentioned in my previous article, I found myself in a sort of "holding area" where patients are prepared for surgery. Each person had their own personal cubicle, and there must have been about ten of us all total. As soon as one left, another was wheeled in. I got to know everyone, and I felt it my duty to welcome them all, to make them feel at home and to comfort them. Finally, a nurse suggested I go back to my own space and "try to calm down." Shucks, I did not mind one bit. They were all so busy, I just wished I had been able to serve punch and cookies.

Then some clown handed me an adorable little cotton gown to put on and tie in the back. Right! There was no way that was going to happen. It must have come from pediatrics because it lacked about two feet of material where it was supposed to meet. My daughters were still with me at this point, and do you think they were any help?? They were practically hysterical watching me struggle with the problem. All I could do was lie flat on my back and pray no one asked me to move!

That would have solved the problem except the moment I was pushed into surgery another comedian told me to "inch" myself off of my stretcher onto another one he was going to hold steady.

Can you get a mental picture of this? I'm trying desperately to hold this stupid gown together and at the same time move myself from one place to another with some degree of modesty and dignity. Needless to say, the shot had begun to wear off and I was not a "happy camper" any longer. I was, however, thankful my daughters were not getting this activity on video. They could have won first place selling it to "Funniest Home Movies," and would not have hesitated to do so.

Obviously, I was then given another shot because the next thing I knew I was back in my room with the girls standing over me, assuring me I was fine . . . easy for them to say. They had not just had a twenty pound pacemaker planted in their chest with a post hole digger!

Almost immediately, a nurse (who I considered a friend) came in to tell me not to get up for any reason for several hours. I said, "You mean except to go to the bathroom."

"I mean NOT FOR ANY REASON "
You are kidding.
"I am NOT kidding."
I can't use a bedpan!
"You CAN use a bedpan."
I won't use a bedpan!
"You WILL use a bedpan!"
I'll stay in bed until I explode!

At this point she smiled sweetly and as she walked out of the room she replied, "Whatever."

Later the doctor, not quite as handsome as before the operation, but still too good looking for me to want to cause any worry, came in to see if I was in much discomfort.

I assured him I was fine, but as soon as I knew he was out of hearing range, I hit the nurse call button and yelled, "I WANT SOMETHING FOR PAIN **NOW**!"

People have asked me how I can write so blatantly about my doctors' good looks. Well, heavens to Betsy, I'm old enough to be their grandmother, but that doesn't mean I'm deaf, dumb and blind!!

WHERE IS F. LEE BAILEY WHEN YOU NEED HIM?

I have always thought of policemen as my friends. I taught my children to think of them as friends. It has never occurred to me that they are not our friends. In fact, it always comes as a big shock when I realize some people don't like me . . . especially one policeman.

I had to accept this fact recently when I ran through a stop sign. I'm not going to deny it. I ran through a stop sign deliberately. It shouldn't be there! I NEVER stop for it. I've lived in this neighborhood for fifteen years, and I have never stopped for it. No one has ever said anything to me before. Of course, I have never hit a police car before either. That might have aggravated the situation a tad!

Several days ago I drove through the same stop sign I have ignored for the past fifteen years I have resided in this neighborhood. Just at I passed the corner, I caught a glimpse of the patrol car obviously hoping for some unsuspecting soul like myself to make some slight mistake. (I call this entrapment.) Thinking I would correct the problem, and at the same time possibly amuse the officer, I put on my brakes and began to back up so I could stop as I should have in the first place. How was I to know he had already pulled up behind me? I backed right into his car. The damage was really quite minor, but I could tell from his expression he was NOT amused. In fact, I feel safe in saying he probably was not an easy person to amuse under any circumstances.

"Could I see your driver's license, please?"

Certainly.

"I mean now!"

You can't see it right now.

"Why?"

I don't have it with me, but I can run home and get it in just a few seconds.

"Why don't you have it with you?"

I'm afraid I'll lose it.

"Ma'am, you are supposed to have it with you at all times."

No one ever told me that before.

"It's in every driver's manual."

How can I get a driver's manual?

"You got one when you applied for your license."

Young man, that has been over fifty years ago.

"The law hasn't changed."

His neck seemed to be turning a deep shade of pink as he began writing out a ticket.

I really don't want a ticket.

"Then you shouldn't have run the stop sign."

I didn't see it.

"Why not?"

I don't have my glasses.

"Your eyesight is so poor you can't see something as large as a stop sign, and you are driving without your glasses?"

Yes, but it's not my fault.

"I can't wait to hear this."

I looked outside and two precious little squirrels were sitting in my feeders.

"So . . . "

So, I didn't have any corn in the feeders, and they were ready to eat.

"I'm not believing this."

I left the house in such a hurry I forgot my glasses.

"I'm sure the judge will understand all of this much better than I
  can."
A two-year old could understand better than you do.
"You don't understand. I'm just doing my job."
Then I suggest you get a REAL job.

At this point his face went from red to purple as he tore out the
ticket and handed it to me. Stomping back to his car I could have
sworn he mumbled something about dealing with old ladies.

My children tell me to just pay the fine without trying to talk to the
judge. Otherwise they are afraid I might have to serve time. What is
this world coming to when a helpless old lady can't try to defend
herself?

Who's Boss? Who Dat, Dat's Who!

Last year I decided it was time to visit my daughter and her family in McComb, Mississippi. This happens to be one of the places I can get to by myself. I have memorized the way if I go on the Natchez Trace. I only make three turns, one onto the Trace, another when I get into Jackson, Mississippi, and then straight on to McComb.

Most folks laugh when I tell them I go that way, but I truly enjoy the scenery, especially in the fall. Mother Nature has started redecorating the trees with gorgeous shades of orange, red and gold, and as I listen to my new Dino tape or one of Andrew Lloyd Webber, I can almost float away mentally in a state of bliss. For about an hour I feel calm and relaxed and the world doesn't seem quite so rough around the edges.

It's a thrill as I drive up honking the horn and see the entire family rush out waving excitedly. (They wave good bye just as excitedly when I leave about a week later.)

The family consists of my daughter and her husband, my grandchildren, Jessica and Katie; two dogs, Who-Dat and Molly; and the cat, Noodles.

Jessica is the oldest granddaughter and I've always called her "Cupcake" because she is so wonderfully sweet. Katie, my namesake, is in the first grade and is special and cute and has more energy than you can imagine, much to the distress of her teacher. This is the child who, when her mother called her to get up the second day of school cried, "You mean I have to go back AGAIN?" My life would be extremely dull without my grandchildren.

Following the usual hugs and kisses, and my son-in-law taking all the luggage in for me, my daughter and I had our cup of coffee. Then

-39-

the girls and I decided to walk to get the kinks out of my old joints. We also decided to take Who-Dat with us. I have no earthly reason why I let the grandchildren talk me into these things. You would think by now I would have learned better. Be that as it may, as we started off I was convinced we must have looked like a Norman Rockwell painting. A grandmother, two beautiful grandchildren and the dog on a leash strolling happily through the neighborhood. We may have looked that way as we started our walk, but it was a different story on our way back!

We had not gotten out of the driveway very far when Who-Dat decided to show me who was boss. Our roles were suddenly reversed. I was no longer walking the dog — the dog was walking me. No, running me would be a better word. The girls were laughing so hard they could hardly walk! I was just a trifle perturbed. I have always felt that if you speak to a dog in a low, but very firm voice, that it will obey. Obviously, this only applies to dogs of normal intelligence. I began to wonder if I would ever get my little entourage back home!

Then, as if things weren't bad enough, a dumb cat prissed slowly in front of us. Well, naturally Who-Dat took the bait and off we went. I know that cat did it on purpose. It was too well timed not to have been deliberate. This was on a Saturday morning when most decent folks are sleeping late, watching cartoons with their children, playing golf, or at the grocery store, not THESE people! They are ALL out in their front yards. NO ONE missed the sideshow. When the leash wrapped around my legs I fell like a ton of bricks. By now, the girls were crying because they thought I had been hurt seriously. I wanted to cry from embarrassment, and Who-Dat was still having the time of his life.

With the girls doing the best they could to help me walk, we did manage to get back to the house. My son-in-law helped me in, my daughter made me sit in the recliner and the children were bringing Band-Aids for all the boo-boos. I had removed most of the top layer of skin from both palms, both knees and both elbows. I did everything that a nurse in the neighborhood suggested, with the exception of my knees. I simply could not figure out a way to soak them in a pan of hot water!

History Repeats Itself
(Invariably)

I seem to get confused more and more, especially when I travel out of town alone. There are two very logical reasons, and I have discussed them with you before. Memory and sense of direction — I no longer have either one. As a result I get lost a lot; I don't mind so much since I meet such nice people when I stop for directions. Besides, I refuse to give up my independence. My daughter always says, "Mother, please wait until I can take you." She says this because she loves me, and because she forgets who is the mother and who is the child. When I decide to go out of town, then I'll go. Of course I always live to regret it. But at least I have proven who is boss.

Remember I wrote about my trip to McComb, Mississippi, several weeks ago? Remember I bragged about how well I made the trip? Well, that was true GOING . . . COMING HOME was an entirely different story.

My son-in-law told me to watch for the Lakeland exit and after turning there I would be back on Highway 25. I thought I saw the sign and I thought I turned correctly, but then I saw another sign that said McComb. I am not the brightest person in the world, but I knew immediately that something was not quite right. McComb was where I had BEEN, not where I wanted to GO. Knowing that the further I drove the more confused I could become, I spotted a large building ahead and to the right. I felt that surely someone there could direct me back to where I was supposed to be.

It was the Veterans Hospital. A very big hospital, a very busy hospital, with so many cars it required a policeman to direct and keep all the traffic moving smoothly.

I pulled up in the loading zone and called to him that I needed help. He just motioned me on. I called to him again, and he continued to motion me to move. He was a very big policeman. He appeared to be a very impatient policeman. When I continued to just sit and look at him, he stopped both lanes of traffic to walk over to my car and said, "Lady, you are blocking traffic and you must move on."

I agreed with him but explained that I couldn't. He wanted to know why and asked if I was ill. I said no, I was simply lost, and I needed to know where to go. Some old man in another car overheard that remark and yelled he would LOVE to tell me where to go.

I am sure the policeman could see a riot in the making, so he told me to pull over to the curb and as soon as he could get traffic moving again, he would be back to help.

As I sat in front of the Veteran's Hospital patiently waiting for the policeman to get a free moment, Mother Nature decided to complicate my life even further. I had to find a ladies room immediately. I motioned for him to come over to my car again. I saw him roll his eyes toward heaven. He slowly put one hand up to stop the right lane of traffic, then slowly put the other hand up to stop the left lane. Then he walked over to me, rested his arm on top of the car, leaned over to look directly into my eyes and said, "What?"

I felt positive I could detect just a touch of impatience in his voice, so I explained the problem and asked sweetly if I could just leave my car parked for about five minutes, long enough to run inside. He replied, "Absolutely not!"

I want to share something with the men reading this article: God has equipped women with a special mechanism to use when all other powers of persuasion fail us. We can cry at the drop of a hat! I cried then. Even while crying I managed to mumble something about police brutality. It did not get the results I had hoped for. He just shook his head in disbelief, but then said he would give me five minutes to get back, or my car would be towed away and I would be arrested.

My feet hardly touched the ground as I dashed madly inside, up one hall and down another. Finally, I saw a sign that said "Ladies." I also saw that half of the women in Jackson were before me. About

20 minutes later I took my time getting back since I knew the car would be gone, and I would be headed for jail. Imagine my thrill to find it still where I had left it. He had been so busy trying to get the traffic jam moving again he had not even noticed how long I had been gone.

Finally, he walked back to my car and asked, "Well, are WE going to move now, or do WE have another problem?" I explained I didn't know about him, but I still was lost. After trying to give me verbal instructions and trying to draw me a map, he must have noticed my eyes were beginning to glaze over. Taking out his walkie-talkie I heard him call for someone to bring the patrol car to the front entrance.

Well, I knew from watching television that I would be allowed one phone call; I decided to use it to let Linda know I would be a little late for supper. Like maybe thirty days.

Then, miracle of all miracles, I heard him tell the second policeman that I was so lost, so confused and so nervous, that he was afraid to turn me loose in traffic. I want you to know that I was led out of Jackson. The patrol car did not leave me until he knew I was headed in the right direction. He even waved as he motioned me on.

My daughter said the family would be so embarrassed to know I had to be escorted out of Jackson by the police. Trying never to be at a loss for words, I replied I had nearly been arrested. Surely they would have been more embarrassed bailing me out of jail.

Ah, Wilderness

If you know anything at all about my family, you know that my father was a very special man. In fact, we sort of like to think of him in Heaven, helping God run things. Anything Paw Paw liked, we liked. Anything he wanted to do, we wanted to do. Any place he wanted to go, we wanted to go. Do you get the picture?

Paw Paw loved camping. He took mother and they went often. My sister and her family usually went with them. My family and I usually stayed home. I decided that was going to change, so the next time they planned a trip I told him we were going too. I noticed some hesitation on his part, and he immediately began telling me all about the discomfort; the bugs, the heat, the sleeping on the hard ground in sleeping bags, and anything else he could dream up in hopes of discouraging us. You see, my idea of "roughing" it was to run out of hot water while taking a shower. BUT nothing deterred us; we were going.

Everyone else left early Saturday morning, but we told them to go on, we would follow as soon as we got everything in the car. With four daughters that meant a lot of clothes, hair dryers, favorite pillows, cosmetics and snack foods. Dad had suggested packing clothes in large paper bags since we could cram more into the trunk that way. We felt that was silly since everything would be all wrinkled. The girls wanted to look nice even when camping.

The trip to Eureka Springs included going through some Arkansas mountains. My third daughter, Diane, took one look out of the window and saw we were very far up, the ground was very far down, and we were on the very edge. She immediately crouched down on the floor of the car and screamed at the top of her voice she wanted to go home. She screamed this without taking a breath for what seemed like an eternity.

As if this was not enough to contend with, my two older girls had decided around the age of twelve or thirteen that one could not touch the other. Since they slept together, this meant an imaginary line had been drawn down the middle of the bed and neither dared to cross it. The same rule applied in the car. I still break out in a cold sweat when I remember my husband trying desperately to find our camp site before dark with one child still screaming she wanted to go home and the other yelling at me to make her sister quit touching her.

Reaching our destination at long last, we began unpacking and I tried to help my husband put up the tent. Just a tiny bit short of patience, he finally reminded me that he had put up and taken down more tents while in the Army than he cared to remember, and didn't I think I could find something else to do, like get the fire started and cook supper.

It was just about this time that my second daughter announced that she needed to find a bathroom. She said she couldn't wait to soak in a hot tub of water for about an hour. Heavens to Betsy, was she in for a shock!

With a smile on his face, Dad pointed in the general direction and she and I started off to find it.

Our idea of a bathroom was a tiled room with hot and cold running water, about ten by twenty feet large, with a tub and shower, a commode that flushes, and plenty of privacy. The authorities who design and oversee the building of these campgrounds have other ideas. They use an empty refrigerator carton, stand it on end and cut a door in one side. There is a seat with a hole in the top, no hot or cold water, no windows and plenty of spider webs and spiders in every nook and cranny. More importantly, there is NO VENTILATION WHATSOEVER, AND IF YOU HAVE EVER BEEN IN ONE OF THESE torture chambers, you know they need LOTS AND LOTS of ventilation.

Well, we stomped back to the camp site and asked where the real bathroom was. Dad nearly doubled over laughing and said between gasps that that WAS the bathroom. He said if we didn't like that one, we could go in the woods. "The wooden what?" asked my daughter, and he laughed even harder. Finally, she knew she had to make a choice and opted for the refrigerator box. Things continued to go down hill from that point in time, and now we had two daughters crying to go home. Still determined to be happy campers, we said we were going to stay, and what's more, we were going to have fun if it killed us. It nearly did!

After dark, we all got our bedrolls situated and soon began to drift off to sleep. Suddenly my first daughter sat straight up and screamed there was a bear outside trying to get in the tent. Discovering it was only a possum, we tried to get settled down again, only to notice a very bad smell. After searching diligently for the cause, we came to the conclusion we had put our tent up right on top of a "pile" left by some animal. Let me tell you, there was no more trying to sleep that night. The girls were ALL crying to go home, I didn't care if we ever went camping for the entire rest of my life, my husband was mad at us all and announced we were heading home the minute he had enough light to find the road back to the highway.

I have thought a lot about the things people do trying to have fun. I can usually find a reason for most of them. Not camping! Why would anyone in their right mind want to leave a comfortable home to be uncomfortable, to leave air-conditioning to be miserably hot, abandon all the creature comforts such as hot and cold running water, and give up a mattress for the ground? Why do they relinquish all privacy and pretend they love it? I KNOW WHY. They are sick in the head. It's their way of crying out for help.

Dad never suggested we go camping again and it's a good thing. I no longer cared if the rest of the family left without us. I was glad. Do you hear? I WAS GLAD. So was Dad . . .

TWO, FOUR, SIX, EIGHT, WHO DO WE APPRECIATE

Haven't I admitted I am not very smart? Over and over again I have confessed to that condition. However, there are some things in life that are deliberately made complicated by "smart" people that could otherwise be quite simple, football being a case in point.

First of all, let me get something off my chest that has been bothering me for some time. Blaming the coach for what the players do is really asinine. In fact, you not only blame him, some of you get down right cranky. Just think of how that must make him feel. It's not fair and it's not nice.

I have been to three games with my daughter, so I am not totally ignorant of the facts. I can see what goes on and it worries me. Those players should be relaxed and rested before the game starts. Instead, what do they do? Well, I'll tell you what they do. They are allowed to dash madly out onto the field like their jerseys are on fire, screaming and carrying on something awful. Heavens to Betsy, those boys are exhausted before the whistle ever blows. I recommend at least thirty minutes of quiet time before each game. They should be required to sit in a room with subdued lighting, talk nicely to each other in soft voices and listen to a tape that will let them experience the tranquillity of the ocean, soothing sounds of a celestial harp, birds singing in the background, and perhaps even the sounds of a gentle rain.

Another thing! You know the young man who runs around the entire field carrying that huge flag? That JUST BREAKS MY HEART. What on earth has he done to deserve that kind of punishment? Surely one other boy could help him, or at least allow him to walk fast.

Has it ever occurred to anyone that the reason the players often do not run as well as they should is because of the weight of their uniforms? I KNOW it is to keep them from getting hurt but why let them play so rough? It's unthinkable the way they all jump on the top of the guy on the ground. That has to be about a thousand pounds of flesh, and then we cheer when the boy on the bottom has to be carried off the field on a stretcher. The more serious the injuries, the louder we cheer!

Now about the goal posts. Someone needs to suggest that when a player has the ball he should run to whichever goal post is the closest. I mean, a post is a post, and they would stand a whole lot better chance of making it.

Referees! They are far too judgmental. I actually think they live to catch a player making a mistake. The penalties are ridiculous. So what if the ball is dropped once in a while? It isn't the end of the world, you know. Why can't he pick it up again, or perhaps someone could be nice enough to hand it to him and let him keep running.

I firmly believe half time should be divided into three parts. That way, we would have something to look forward to, and the time would really pass a lot quicker.

In closing, I would like to suggest one more thing. It should be required of anyone buying a ticket to agree to stay and cheer our boys on until the end of the game, EVEN, if they did not score a single point! They played didn't they? They could have been studying. The least we could do is show our appreciation.

Cinderella at the Orpheum

Doubtless I have mentioned that we enjoy live stage productions. We have been to the New Stage Theater in Jackson, Mississippi, the Orpheum in Memphis, Tennessee, and The Saenger in New Orleans, Louisiana. More often than not we go to Memphis since that is where we lived the biggest part of our lives, and we are a little more relaxed about driving. We still get lost, just not as often. But then, I can get lost in my own neighborhood.

Patrons of the arts in Memphis dress pretty much the way they want to dress, other than on opening night performances. You will see both casual and formal attire and lots in between. Because it is an "occasion" for us, we usually go in our Sunday best. Our seats were on the mezzanine but I felt binoculars would ensure a better view so I borrowed a pair. They were a drab shade of green and I'm sure had been used in World War I to spot enemy aircraft.

In spite of the way they looked, I said, "What the heck, no one would see them but me anyway." I was thrilled to have them. At least I was until a beautifully dressed young woman floated in to occupy the seat next to me. She was a vision of loveliness. Chiffon tea-length skirt, sequin covered jacket, satin shoes and last but not least, she held a dainty, gold-trimmed pair of opera glasses. They were so fragile, so tiny, so . . . appropriate, that I immediately wanted to simply vanish. I know it sounds silly to say I was intimidated by a pair of glasses, but I guess you would have had to be there to appreciate the situation.

Well, I looked at her. She looked at me. I glanced at her glasses, and she glanced at mine. I remarked I could see everything on stage clearly. She remarked I should be able to see anywhere in the United States! I asked why with all the hundreds of seats in the Orpheum did she manage to get reservations right next to me? She replied she had just been born unlucky. Then we both got tickled.

Because my binoculars were so heavy (must have weighed ten pounds) I had to rest my arms frequently.

Noticing my discomfort, she graciously suggested that we swap for awhile. Immediately I felt like Cinderella when the pumpkin turned into a wonderful coach, and her rags to a gorgeous gown. I was absolutely BEAUTIFUL . . . no doubt about it. She on the other hand, had become old and ugly and EXTREMELY overdressed!

I Don't Know If I Will
Ever Have Another Chance

I don't know whether to laugh or cry now that deer season is here. Flashbacks from last year make me want to run and hide so my daughter can't find me.

Since her husband is an expert on deer, she tells me this qualifies her automatically as a semi-expert. Like so many other things she tells me, I believe her because I don't know any better.

Living outside the city limits in a wooded area, they see lots of deer. In order to attract them closer to their home, my son-in-law puts corn out about twenty or thirty feet from the back patio. These are "deer" friends invited to dine on corn provided especially for them. In exchange, the family has the pleasure of watching them from close quarters. In other words, they have their own private wildlife show. NO SHOOTING IS EVER ALLOWED!

Now, I may have casually remarked at some point that I would love to see them too, but I certainly do not remember saying it was a matter of life and death. Obviously, she must have THOUGHT I said that because it became her main goal in life to concoct a plan whereby I could have a ringside seat, be warm, be comfortable, enjoy the view and not be seen by the deer. The latter was most important. They won't show if they know people are watching. In order to hide your presence, you have to be absolutely silent.

Now, my daughter should have known that last requirement ensured the plan was doomed from the beginning, since no one in my family is "absolutely silent." She decided we would watch the deer from inside a pup tent. It was designed for a SMALL child, not for two women and a dog.

I know you are wondering where the dog came from. Originally, he came from the dog pound. Someone abandoned him. My daughter wanted a dog and loved "Sam" at first sight. The feeling was mutual. She brought this furry little puppy home, fed him, bathed him, loved him, and saw that he got all the shots necessary to grow strong. Well, he grew and he was strong, but other than eating everything he could find, he was absolutely of no value. He is huge with long black hair. He looks like a bear. He really looks mean but he is scared of his own shadow! I believe he is the dumbest dog on earth, but he loves my daughter with a devotion that is unparalleled. Where she goes, he goes.

When she crawled in the tent, he crawled in behind her. He was uninvited, but made himself comfortable as close to her as he could possibly get. This left precious little room for me. I squeezed in, and sat flat on the ground with legs straight out in front of me. I urge any of you over sixty-five with stiff joints to sit in this position for about thirty minutes. I couldn't straighten up for a week and my knees will never be the same.

It had rained earlier and Sam was still wet. He was so happy to be with us. He was panting and grinning with his tongue hanging out at least a foot. The combination of dog breath and wet dog hair smell was turning the air in that small tent blue. Determined not to offend my daughter or Sam by commenting on the ungodly odor, (after all, wasn't this treat just for my benefit?), I tried breathing through my mouth.

Noticing my discomfort, my daughter pulled a small stool into the tent for me to sit on. Now my head hit the top of the tent and I had to sit bent over to see outside. I honestly don 't know when I have ever been more miserable, but determined to let her show me a good time, even if it killed me, I hid my feelings behind a frozen smile.

By now it was growing dark, she warned me not to move or make a sound and to look closely in the direction of the corn. I did everything she told me to do. Suddenly she whispered something in my ear. I whispered back, "What?" We repeated this scenario several times until in exasperation she hissed rather loudly that the deer were at the corn. Naturally, the deer heard her and disappeared like magic. I never saw a single deer. She saw deer. Sam saw deer. I did not. My daughter called at noon to tell me she has a really special treat planned for me next week. Pray for me. I may not survive another one.

Inferior Decorating At Its Best

Please do not let anyone convince you that it will cost hundreds of dollars to redecorate your home. I am here to tell you that it does not. At least, not if you use just a little imagination and a total lack of good taste.

Waking early one morning several months ago, I stumbled into the kitchen for that first wonderful cup of coffee. Suddenly I stopped and said to myself, "Self, this kitchen needs a complete overhaul." I was looking at the same old cabinets, the same old counter tops that I had been looking at for the past fifteen years. No more! Things were going to change . . .

My first visit was to a local company that handled everything I would need. After getting samples of every possible color and design, I rushed back home to match them with the carpet in the eating area of the kitchen, a royal blue. You see, cleverly, I had already decided not to replace the carpet, simply to use colors that would either match or complement it. There wasn't one. Do you realize how many "blues" there are in the world? Do you also realize how seldom one will blend with the other?

The walls of my kitchen are a sort of sea foam green. I decided to match that instead. Back to the store I went. In fact, I went back to every store in town, several times, with no luck. I went so often that I could see the sales clerks duck behind the counter trying to avoid me. Oh, they pretended they were looking for something. Right! They were looking to see when I would give up and leave.

Eventually one of the stores hired a new sales girl who didn't know me, and she seemed eager to assist me the first time I talked to her. She seemed eager the second time I went in too . . . and the third.

After that, however, she also seemed to spend a lot of time straightening behind the counters.

Well, one day I decided to take another approach to my problem. I couldn't understand why I was having so much trouble. I would love to tell you I have a large home with five bedrooms, a bath in each one, a recreation room, formal dining area, a breakfast nook, a Jacuzzi, and a porch overlooking a lake. What I do have is a three-bedroom house, two of which are the size of closets, the kitchen and eating area are one and the same, a bath and a half, and a garden hose we can turn on guests, if they are into that sort of thing. So you see, my home is as simple as it can be, so why all the problems when I want to brighten things up a bit?

To be frank, I've learned during my many visits to stores that it will cost a small fortune. That's it in a nutshell. So I am back to square one. What to do? I'll do it myself. Other people can. Martha Stewart does it all the time, so why can't I? I'll tell you why. I am not "other people," nor am I Martha Stewart. Frankly, I do not believe she is a real person. No one can possibly be as talented as she is. When does she rest? When does she sleep? When does she prepare meals for her family, make the beds, wash clothes, iron, or even take out the garbage? Where does she even find room to sit down in the middle of all the "stuff" she works with? To put it very bluntly, she makes me sick and tired.

After long and deliberate thought, I decided to simply paint my cabinets white. It made a huge difference. I placed a decorative border above the counters and stove. I moved the toaster from one side of the counter to the other. I put the can opener where the toaster had been. The canisters are where the cookie jar used to sit. I was thrilled with the transformation! When my daughter came for lunch that day, she cried, saying it was not the same anymore. She no longer felt like it was home, she begged me not to change anything else. Guess I'll just forget the new kitchen towels. That might be the very thing that would push her over the edge!

Nobody Knows the Trouble I've Seen

I did promise not to travel out of town alone. I have kept that vow. It has not been easy, but I did it in order that I might have a little peace and quiet in my life again. I don't mind when folks laugh WITH me, but I am a little bit sensitive when they laugh AT me.

It suddenly occurred to me that the only way to prevent ridicule is to "lay low" for a while, at least until everyone tires of talking about my travel experiences. So when the family agreed we would all go to McComb, Mississippi again last week, I naturally was the first to climb in the van. For some strange reason I am always afraid they will pack up and leave without me. My son-in-law says I have good reason to feel that way.

The most recent trip was planned so we could see the beautiful Easter pageant First Baptist Church in McComb was putting on. (My daughter was in it, so that made it even more beautiful. Other mothers will understand that remark.)

I have to admit it was wonderful to just sit back, relax, and not have to worry about things like detours, highway numbers or exits. I could close my eyes and doze, I could read my new Jan Karon book, or simply listen to the gospel radio station. Everything went as smooth as silk.

After just visiting for a while, we decided to get dressed for the program. Wanting to get to the church in plenty of time to get good seats, we were going to eat early. In order to save even more time, I offered to run to the grocery store for paper plates and cups, eliminating all the kitchen cleanup. Two granddaughters wanted to ride with me.

Still aware of the time element, we rushed in Kroger, we rushed to find what we had come for, we rushed back up front to the check-out, then rushed out to the car . . . and I couldn't find the car keys.

I knew immediately I must have dropped them as I was paying for the merchandise. We rushed back in. Now, I know you think this was too much rushing, but you need to remember we only had about 30 minutes to get back home, eat and get to the church.

I asked the checker if she had found the keys. No luck! I went to the office to see if someone had turned them in. No! The girls looked through my purse again. Time was running out so I asked if I could use their phone to call home. I couldn't remember the number; the manager couldn't find his telephone book. I was really upset about this because if he had been a little more organized that phone book would have been at his fingertips, and I would only have been in half as much trouble.

Returning to the car again to see if I could have possibly dropped them getting out of the car, one of the grandchildren discovered I had locked them in the car.

I beg you to remember that I had felt this trip would go without a single mistake, and as you remember that, try to imagine how I hated to let anyone at home know what had happened. I thought about blaming one of the girls but neither one was old enough to drive. I even thought about saying I was held up at gun point and robbed of the keys, but why would anyone rob me of the keys and then leave the car? Desperate at this point I went into a furniture store, used their telephone book and called home.

The minute my daughter heard my voice, she yelled, "Motherrrr." I could also hear the rest of the family laughing — at MY expense.

"Have you had a wreck?" they would ask.
Of course not.
"Are you lost again?"
No!
"Are you hurt?"
Not at all.
"Are the girls okay?"
They are in perfect condition.

"Why don't you come home?"

I can't.

"Why not?"

The car won't run.

"What's wrong with it?"

I can't drive it from where I'm standing.

"Where are you standing?"

On the outside.

"Well, just get inside the car and come home."

I can't do that either.

"Why not?"

The keys are locked in the car.

There was dead silence for a few seconds, then it sounded as if she was talking through clenched teeth when she said, "Mother, we are supposed to be at the church in 15 minutes."

Several minutes later my son-in-law came skidding into the parking lot on two wheels, used his key to get me in the car, and I tried to look as innocent as possible as I walked into the house with my head held high.

We made it to the cantata by the skin of our teeth, and it was absolutely beautiful. I wouldn't have missed it for anything. (Except, of course, not having any transportation to the church.)

I dreaded the trip home. I knew what I would have to endure all the way back to Starkville, Mississippi, so I concocted what I felt would be the perfect defense. Have you ever PRETENDED to be sound asleep for four hours?

What 'good old days'?

Now, I want to ask a very simple question, and I will appreciate a very simple answer. Am I the only person in the world that knows that the "good old days" were not all that good? You know by now that I tell the truth about things, that I NEVER exaggerate, and that any facts I give in these stories are accurate. What I am going to explain to you today is not fiction. It's the story of my old washing machine, it's death and the memories the event evoked.

Thinking the load I had started in the machine was ready for the dryer, I went to the utility room and found they were sitting in a tub full of water. I punched every button, rearranged the load, and said a few choice words, but the machine would not respond. Rushing to the telephone I called the repair service and asked if they would send someone to revive the stubborn thing, explaining I had clothes still sitting in water.

"What seems to the be the problem with it?"
The problem is it won't work.
"How old is the machine?"
Well, I guess it's close to 17 years old.
"That's pretty old for a washer."
Little lady, some folks think I am pretty old too, but I'm still
    working.
"Are you sure you want to put money in one this old? It could go
    out again any time. Perhaps you might like to consider a new
    one."
All I want to consider is what time today someone will be here.
"Oh, it will be next week before I can get you scheduled."

What am I supposed to do with this load of wet clothes?

"Sometimes, in a case like this, it is necessary to remove them from the machine."

Do you mean by hand?

"Or by foot if you think that would be easier."

I could tell by that remark she was a very impatient employee, so I asked to speak to the supervisor.

"I am the supervisor."

Then you should be able to see that I have an emergency.

"No, ma'am, food about to spoil in a freezer that won't work is an emergency. An air conditioner that isn't working when the temperature is 100 degrees is an emergency."

Now that you mention it, I am afraid my freezer will go out too, so send someone to look at it.

"Is it out yet?"

Not quite.

"Is the food inside beginning to thaw?"

Not yet.

"Then you don't have an emergency, do you?"

Really upset over her attitude, I told her to forget the work order, that I would find someone else. I wish I had not told her that, because four hours later I was still calling repair shops without success.

Knowing that I was about to fall apart, I made myself a cup of coffee and relaxed. I must have dozed off, because I dreamed about wash days when I was a young girl. It was more like a nightmare.

It was my job to help mother on wash days and I hated it worse than liver.

The machine was automatic in that you plugged the cord into the wall socket to get the on and off switch to work. After that, it was all manual. We had to decide when we thought the clothes had washed long enough. Two galvanized tubs sat side by side next to the washer. Both were filled with rinse water. You put a few garments at a time into the wringer (two rollers that squeezed the water out) that was turned by hand. Putting too many in at a time meant they got stuck and wrapped around the wringer. It was no small thing to remove them. The first tub of rinse water was clear, the second had what we called blueing added to it. The wringer was automatic in that it could be repositioned from one tub to another. They had to be put through this contraption by hand, removed by hand and hung outside on the clothes line by hand. The whole process took an entire day, because you must remember there were always several loads of clothes to be done.

I was awakened by the telephone ringing. It was my daughter asking what I had planned for the day. I never hesitated. "I plan to shop for a new washer," I told her. If I couldn't get anyone to fix my old one until next week, I surely was not going to do laundry by hand. The "good old days" were not so good. I have been there, done that. Once was enough.

Hot Under the Collar

I guess I should never have mentioned "the good old days." I should have just forgotten the whole idea. I should learn when to leave well enough along. Yes, and pigs should learn to fly!

I no sooner had taken care of the washing machine situation when my car air-conditioning decided to give up. <u>Thinking</u> it had probably blown a fuse, and <u>thinking</u> I could pick one up at the auto parts store for a few dollars, and <u>thinking</u> my son-in-law could replace it in just a few minutes, I was not too concerned, at least not yet.

Someone noticed my inspection sticker had expired, six months ago so I headed for my favorite auto repair shop, thinking they could replace the fuse at the same time they renewed the sticker.

"You are lucky you haven't been stopped by the police."
For what?
"This sticker has been out for several months."
Well, my car was just inspected last year.
"It's supposed to be replaced each year."
There isn't anything wrong with my car.
"You don't know that unless we inspect it."
Is this just another way to rip off the public?
"No, ma'am, it's a way to keep you and other drivers safe."
I have never had a wreck in my life.
"How old are you , Mrs. Teasley?"
Old enough to know THAT is not an appropriate question.
"I'm just trying to suggest that as we get older our reflexes are not quite so good."
Perhaps yours are not. Mine are fine.

After he replaced the sticker, I pulled the hood and asked him to replace the fuse.

"What fuse?"
The one that works the air conditioning.
"Mrs. Teasley, a fuse is not your problem."
It most certainly is, and I'm about to blow MINE if you don't get my car fixed so I don't die of heat exhaustion.
"The compressor is out. You will have to replace it."
How much will it cost and how long will it take?
"Longer than you will like, and more than you will want to pay."
How do you know that?
"Because I have been dealing with you for a lot of years."
Does that mean you want me to give my business to someone else?
"Heavens, no! What would I do for entertainment?"

After hearing the cost of a rebuilt compressor, I stated flat out I was not going to pay that much, that we never had air-conditioning back in the old days, and I could surely do without one now.

Once again, as in the past, I marched out in a huff, head held high and shoulders back, and determined not to place too much importance on "creature comfort," I headed home. I rolled the windows down to create a breeze and told myself it wasn't going to be so hot after all. That was the first block. The second one I began to get a little warm. By the time I reached home, perspiration was running down my nose and fogging my glasses. I felt as though I had been riding inside a furnace with wheels on it.

While I told myself that hot weather now is a lot hotter than it was in the old days, I also told myself I was going to have to "eat crow" once again. It is now a steady part of my diet. I'm even beginning to like the taste of it. I just hope it's low in calories because I eat it a lot.

As soon as possible I plan to have the air conditioner fixed. I don't mind being a little uncomfortable, but I refuse to die of a heat stroke.

In the meantime, I am praying for an early winter.

W.W.W.W.W.
Club To Be Organized

Many, many years ago when I was in the fifth grade, I had a history teacher named Miss Morrow. She could tell when I walked in the room if I had done my homework or not.

I hated history. I hated Miss Morrow. But the point I am trying to make is if I can remember <u>her</u> so easily, why do I struggle to remember the names of my grandchildren?

Raised in Memphis, Tennessee, as children we often went into town for special events. Back in those days almost every special event took place on Main Street — all the big beautiful theaters, the auditorium, the wonderful parades, etc. Living in East Memphis, we caught the Central Avenue bus, rode to Cooper and Peabody, transferred to the number 2 Fairgrounds streetcar and rode all the way into town for the sum of seven cents.

I remember Bry's, Woolworths, Lowensteins, Gerbers, and Goldsmiths, all in that order. If I can remember the names of those department stores, exactly where they were and how to get there, why do I get lost going to Sturgis?

Ever wonder why Kroger and Food-Max began staying open all night? For me . . . that's why! If I remember to make out a grocery list I forget to take it with me. Friends say I am hard to catch at home. Well, sure I am, I'm always at the grocery store trying to get what I forgot the time before. I want to thank these stores publicly for this consideration. Oh, I'm almost positive anyone can take advantage of this 24 hour program, but as a rule it's only myself and the night crew there.

I have a small problem remembering to enter checks in my check book. There was a time when I could sit down, concentrate for a few minutes and recall where and for how much I had written the missing item. Now I could sit down and concentrate 'til doomsday and forget what I was even trying to remember.

I was forced to call the bank so often they had to hire additional help. Then, they implemented the 24 hour automatic service that tells your balance and the last 10 checks that have cleared. Isn't that just the nicest thing? Thanks, NBC for making me feel so special!

The last problem I want to discuss is really very personal and to tell the truth, I'm embarrassed to share it with you. I lose my car every time I shop at Wal-Mart! Now, I am an old lady, I don't have many miles left in me, and I'm using them all up hunting MY OWN CAR! I love Wal-Mart. I depend on Wal-Mart, but some day I am going to get lost in that parking lot and no one will ever try to find me. I need help.

I am exhausted from walking up one row and down another with a vacant look on my face, trying to pretend I know where I parked. Couldn't some sort of transportation be provided to drive confused customers around until they spot their cars? It could be a horse drawn wagon for all I care.

Friends, we need to unite. The problem of trying to remember who, what, when, where, and why is universal among older people. We need assistance. We need understanding and we need our own support group!

Our first meeting will be at the Greensboro Center on the 9th of October at 7 o'clock or is it on the 7th of October at 9 o'clock. Whatever . . . please make plans to be there.

This Writer's Middle Name
Ain't Stupid

Part I

I am the first to admit I have a few shortcomings. However, one thing I am NOT is gullible. You would have to get up pretty early in the morning to get ahead of Edith Teasley.

As an example: false advertising. I can spot it a mile away. All of the over-the-counter pain killers claim to the be very best.

Ha!

Each one says hospitals use theirs the most.

And these "doctors" on TV who pose on the edge of their desks and talk to us in their most confidential manner are not doctors at all. You see? I am not easily misled. If I do say so myself, I am pretty dog-gone sharp.

Having said all of this, I feel it is only fair of me to apologize to the Publisher's Clearinghouse. I have been too hasty in shrugging them off as just another ruse to make money off unsuspecting people. This fine group of workers is on the up and up.

Previously, I have taken a dim view of everything they have done. (I still take a dim view of those spots on TV where the van drives up to a house, a beautiful girl wrapped in only a towel comes to the door to be told she has just become a millionaire, some other lady keeps yelling, "You have got to be kidding," and still another just rolls her eyes and exclaims, "Oh, no!")

I wish they would cut all that out. It hurts their credibility.

Now, for the first time, I have started actually reading the material that comes through the mail, and I am <u>convinced</u> they are legitimate.

The first was a post card addressed to me personally, telling me that after careful consideration of all my excellent qualifications, they were going to send a special package that would arrive on December 26. It came just as promised.

The card also went on to warn me not to be fooled by imitators. I truly appreciated the thought but, hey, I didn't just fall off the back of a turnip truck, you know. I'm pretty hard to fool.

That is exactly why I know that "Dave" has to be, without a doubt, the sweetest, kindest, most considerate man on the face of this earth. I just can't wait to meet him in person.

Oh, he hasn't come right out and PROMISED me I will win, but I just know <u>he</u> knows I have a really good chance. Why else would he ask me to let him know where I would be, if I don't plan to be home on Super Bowl Sunday?

You should see some of the other things he wrote in this letter. I even received a form to fill out giving my approval for a live TV announcement at my address.

Some man named Todd is going to tell the world that the winner lives in Starkville, Mississippi. Another person will be shown congratulating me for winning the $10 million. Then, now get this, THEN I will say to the whole world, "I can't believe it. I guess I am rich now."

This is the only part of the scenario that I don't like, and I plan to call Todd (I have his personal 800 number) and suggest just a few changes.

Maybe I should call Dave since he is actually the executive director of the prize control. It probably doesn't matter which one I call. They are both personal friends now and we are on a first-name basis with each other. It makes it so much easier to communicate this way.

There is one thing I have promised myself, and I hasten to promise all my friends . . . I will still be the same down-to-earth person that I have always been. I don't plan to change my lifestyle ONE LITTLE BIT. My front door will always be open to you.

Above all, I am not counting my chickens before they hatch. I understand that I MAY NOT be the winner.

However, just to be on the safe side, I plan to hire an architect to draw up some plans for a much larger home. I need more room when the children come to visit, and for the entertaining I plan to do . . . as soon as I return from my trip around the world.

If I am not home when you drop by, just leave your calling card with the butler . . .

Part II

The clock is ticking. Each day brings me closer and closer to the biggest day of my life — announcing to the world the fact that I am the million dollar winner. However, each time I hear from the Publisher's Clearinghouse, I feel more strongly than the time before, that I actually have a very, very good shot at winning. I also feel they are trying their best to let me know it without coming right out and saying so. Call it a woman's intuition if you like. One member of my family called it stupidity, but then there are always a few skeptics in any situation.

One of the few things Publisher's Clearinghouse has asked me to do, and Heavens to Betsy it's little enough, is to order magazines at a greatly reduced price to help offset the cost of their program. Well, I ordered quite a few some weeks back, trying to save coupons and to tell you the truth, I don't even read the ones that come regularly now. In fact, I have magazines stacked to the ceiling in my spare bedroom. I searched and searched for one or two I don't already have, and all I can come up with is "100 Assorted Baseball Cards, Rookies and Stars" or another called "Car Driver." I can always use them to start a fire in the fireplace. (I don't have a fireplace now, but I will have in my new home.)

You see, I am really trying very hard to keep both feet planted firmly on the ground and plan ahead. You often hear stories about people who suddenly become wealthy and do all sorts of crazy things. Not me. In fact, I have hired a personal financial planner to guide and advise me AHEAD OF TIME in order to avoid the pitfalls of suddenly becoming rich. I'm also considering hiring a secretary for the financial planner, so he can devote all of his energies to my future security. Nothing foolish or unnecessary; I am keeping a level head about my situation. I may even write a book and call it, "A Guide To Being Wealthy Suddenly and Remaining Humble."

There are only a few more days until the big announcement. I want all of you to know, YOU are invited to the party. Please dress casual; I have never been a formal person, and I don't intend to let wealth turn me into a pretentious human being.

Part III

I am a very level-headed person. I am fair-minded, not given to excesses or blind rage, nor do I resent another person's good fortune. At the same time, let me add that I do not laugh at another person's misfortune. However, I have never said my feelings cannot be hurt. I am just as sensitive as the next fellow, and those of you who insist on calling to ask if I have received the million dollars yet need to get a life. On the other hand, if it gives you some sort of perverse pleasure to ridicule me for being a trusting person, then go ahead, have your fun.

Someone just called wanting to sell me the Brooklyn Bridge. Now THAT is really hurtful. Don't they think I KNOW the shipping alone on that thing would cost a fortune?

Still another called and asked if I'd like to lecture on how to get rich the hard way, then hung up laughing.

After giving my situation very careful thought (as you know by now I give every situation very careful thought), I decided to call the Better Business Bureau.

I want to report a severe case of fraud.
"I've heard of a severe case of measles, but never a severe case of fraud."
Well, you've heard of it now, because that is exactly what I mean.
"This complaint needs to be submitted in writing."

I don't have time for that, someone else could be hurt.

"If you've been hurt you need to call the police."

They are still mad at me for running a stop sign.

"You should know better than to run a stop sign."

I DO now.

"Perhaps you should call the FBI. They have more man-power and will be better able to address your problem."

You haven't even asked what the problem is yet.

"That's because I'm afraid to."

Realizing I was not going to receive the help I so desperately needed, I called the FBI and explained the company had promised that I'd be a millionaire, only I wasn't.

"Did they promise or just say you COULD be?"

They said I could be.

"There is no crime in that."

But I ordered magazines.

"Did they force you to order them?"

No, but they said it would help them a lot.

"And I am sure that it did."

It's really hard to explain so you will understand.

"Just take your time ma'am. I don't have anything better to do than listen to this ridiculous story."

At this display of kindness I simply lost control. It was as though the tailgates had opened and a flood of tears gushed forth. I guess you could say it was the straw that broke the horse's back.

Thank you so much. You are a wonderful human being. You must have a wonderful mother.

"Is there anything else?"

Yes, half of Starkville, Mississippi, came to my celebration party.

"That was nice of you."

Everyone is laughing at me.

"There is no crime in that either."

Are you going to stop them or not.

"Who? The people who are laughing?"

No, the ones who said I would be a millionaire.

"It would be easier to stop the ones laughing."

So, OK, maybe I was a little foolish. Maybe I didn't get rich. Money isn't everything. Money is the root of all evil. Money can't buy happiness. A good name is better than gold.

SOME people never grow up. SOME remain immature all their lives. SOME are so childish they enjoy trying to make me feel badly. All I've got to say to them is: Sticks and stones may break my bones, but words will never hurt me.

Thanks for the Memories

As I reflect back to the first time I was told I was expecting a baby, a full range of emotions come into play, just as they did that day.

First of all I was scared. Back then, most young women, even married ones, did not know all about pregnancy. Today of course, we know all there is to know. I just knew I was scared. My doctor said not to worry, it was perfectly normal and I wouldn't remember a thing after it was all over. Biggest lie a doctor ever told.

Second, I was surprised. Why? Well, that's easy to explain. You see my husband and I had discussed "a family" and decided to wait until we were on our feet financially. Besides, mother always said I could do anything I made up my mind to do and I had decided not to get in the "family way." Yes, that's what we called it back in those days. The word pregnant was far too personal. That alone might give you some idea of how stupid I really was. Nevertheless, in my family, we were not allowed to use certain words that referred to the anatomy. Another example, we could not ask for a chicken breast at the table. We had to say we preferred a piece of white meat.

As the weeks passed, even I knew something was not quite right. Primarily because of the round tummy that was developing. At the doctor's office I was met with some degree of skepticism.

The nurse asked me out loud if I was expecting.

Expecting what?
"A baby."
Of course not.
"Why not?"
Because I can't possibly be . . . you know, that way.

I remember she patted me on the shoulder as if I was not very bright, shook her head sadly and said the doctor would be right in.

Then I had to go through pretty much the same routine with the doctor.

"The nurse tells me you said you could not possibly be pregnant."
That is absolutely correct.
"I suggest you think back and try to remember a night that might possibly hold an explanation."
I am a very sound sleeper and never remember anything.
"How exciting that must be for your husband."
Well, he always seems happy just to know I have a pulse. Besides, doctor, we are not ready for children, yet.
"Then I suggest you go home and get ready."

Of course, as you have already guessed. I was definitely in the "family way," no ifs, ands, or buts.

I told my husband the minute he walked in the door. He was so proud it was unbelievable. He was just as proud three more times during our married life. We had four of the most loving daughters in the world.

I think for Mother's Day I will fix the children's favorite casserole. It calls for six boned chicken brea . . chicken brea . . . a lot of white meat.

Grandmother and Granddaughter
Share Some Special 'Pillow Talk'

Born May 11, 1970, Patricia was a grandmother's dream come true. A head full of black hair, round fat little cheeks, chubby legs, and the biggest brown eyes I had ever seen. After showing her to everyone through the big glass window, the nursery lady motioned me aside and let me hold this "doll" in my arms for a few seconds. I know we bonded for life at that very moment, and we have been very close ever since. From the very beginning Tricia has been close to perfection, as far as her grandmother is concerned.

I have to admit there was a period when she did not exercise the best judgment in the world, but then, who does when they are three years old? Let me elaborate . . .

It was never meant for me to be a seamstress. I have five thumbs on both hands. I have wasted more time and destroyed more good fabric trying to sew than you would ever believe. I even need instructions to thread a needle. Nevertheless, about every three or four years I forget I can't sew and I get the urge to create something out of material. As soon as I held Tricia, I knew deep down in my heart I had to make her something special with my own hands. A pillow! What could be simpler?

I did not do anything fancy, but every stitch was made with love. She latched onto it immediately. They were inseparable. Where she when, it went. Any other woman would have been ashamed to admit she had made it. Tricia carried this pillow around until it was no more than a piece of ragged looking material with only three or four cotton balls in one corner. Friends asked us who made it. We said we didn't remember. They asked what it was. We said we didn't know. Some asked why we didn't take it away from her. We invited them to try.

I remember the night we decided to wean her away from this pathetic-looking "thing." It really was a source of embarrassment.

Her other grandmother, known for her handiwork, had made several really beautiful little pillows. So far, they were used to decorate the room and Tricia's baby bed. They WERE beautifully made. Up until the night Tricia lost her old "piddow" (as she pronounced it), these pretty ones had never been functional. NOW we felt positive we could make the switch as the old one had been misplaced.

Searching in vain every place we could think of until almost midnight, we began offering Tricia one of the pretty ones. There was not going to be any sleeping for anyone until she accepted one of them. As fast as her mother handed her one, we would see it fly through the air out into the hall with Tricia screaming bloody murder. Finally, in desperation, I rushed home to find an old slip which I cut up, placed about four cotton balls down in one corner, stitched it together and took it back to my granddaughter. I will never forget the satisfied look on her little face as she wrapped it around her thumb, began rubbing the side of her face with it, and instantly, with a look of utter contentment, she fell fast asleep.

This particular "piddow" set the pattern for all future ones. They had to be soft silky material with no more than four cotton balls in one corner. Tricia knew immediately if one was not made correctly, and would refuse to accept it. I saved any and all old slips and purchased a bag of cotton balls that would last for years. Her pillows were misplaced many times, but I had learned to keep several on hand for emergencies. I was really proud that my pillows were so special to her. Many friends very sweetly offered to make a "real" pillow, and we graciously allowed them to do so, knowing all along that Tricia would not use them. Over the years we had a large assortment of pillows, but none were ever used to calm and soothe my little granddaughter except mine.

The second time Tricia lost her pillow was the first time she ever ran away from home. Hearing a strange noise at my front door one evening, I opened it to find her standing there holding her old teddy bear by the ear, tears running down her cheeks and nose red from crying. She had lost her pillow again. Bringing her inside, I hurriedly found one of the extras and took her back home. This was the first of several "run-aways." None of us were ever concerned; she always ran to my house, and I lived just next door.

The Importance of Educational TV

Yes! I am on another soap box. Why do I continue to do it? Well, it's an ugly business and someone has to do it.

I am tired of being left out of things. I want to play too. Just because I, and many others in my age bracket, have some extra mileage on us and more birthday candles on our cakes, does not mean we should be put out to pasture. I am once again asking for some support, friends. Those of you who feel as I do, must speak up. We will raise our voices in unison to bring about a change in the way society feels about senior citizens.

You want to know what brought all this about? I'll be more than happy to tell you what brought it all about . . . everything is geared toward young people. Well, WE ARE STILL HERE, and frankly we hope to be around for ten or fifteen more years. What are we supposed to do, twiddle our thumbs? Talk about our health and our aches and pains? Compare prescriptions?

Do you ever wonder why we get so cranky? WE DON'T HAVE ANY FUN. Society worries about kids and what they do in their spare time. How about worrying about all OUR spare time. Frankly, we watch a lot of TV, we wait for the Modern Maturity magazine each month, and we get REALLY excited when the postcard comes from an insurance company reminding us how much a funeral service costs. THAT one always makes my day brighter.

Speaking of TV, THIS is the subject I intended to expand on today. To be more specific, the models used in commercials. Where are the older people?

Exercise equipment ads always use people who have never even gotten up to normal weight for their height. They don't need to lose inches; if they turned sideways they would be invisible.

Then we come to the commercial using two beautiful young people dining by candlelight. Of course they look beautiful. Anyone looks better in candle light. Myself, I look even better in no light at all.

However, I digress. The point I am trying to make is that they should have — indeed they COULD have — used an older couple. Just think of the influence it might have on some senior citizens. Television ads need to encompass a larger audience, ads that will target those who have reached their golden years. I can just see it now . . .

The little wife, wearing her prettiest apron over her flannel bathrobe, fuzzy slippers slapping against the bare floor, and wearing an artificial flower in her hair, has decided to follow the example of the couple in the commercial. She lights candles placed in the center of the table and calls for her husband to come eat. So far, on this particular day, all he has said to her is "You know I don't like my oatmeal this thick," "Where is the paper?" and "When do we eat?"

Now, he struggles to his feet, waits a few seconds to get his legs steady, and walks away from the never-ending checkers game he plays with his neighbor. His stomach hangs over his wrinkled jeans, he hasn't shaved in three days, and has a wad of tobacco in his jaw that could choke a horse. THEN he notices the candles.

They gaze across the table into each other's eyes. Suddenly, Paw reaches across a bowl of steaming turnip greens and a plate of hot cornbread, and tenderly takes her hand.

I don't know how this scenario ends, but I do know Paw hasn't been this excited in twenty years, and as he leads her from the table, Maw thinks she had died and gone to heaven.

Mirror, Mirror on the Wall

I hope you all noticed that I made no New Year's resolutions. Reason? Simple! I never keep them; no one does. This year I just sat back and laughed at those of you who promised to either give up something or change something. Case in point, more often than not it is smoking or food. However, getting a really good view of myself in a full-length mirror while trying on clothes recently was quite a shock. You see, I have all the mirrors in my house covered half way down. Seeing the top half is bad enough. Seeing the bottom half destroyed me emotionally. I made a mad dash home, jumped into bed, pulled the covers up over my head and cried bitter tears for the rest of the day. I even wondered why the children let me go out in public. Finally, I pulled myself together and resolved to lose weight — again!

We all know there are two ways to get rid of extra pounds — eat less and exercise more. Well, I am not stupid. I know from past experience that I WILL eat whatever I want. You would not believe the devious ways I can get food into my mouth, even while claiming to be on a strict diet. For instance, when I cook. How can any hostess serve food that she does not know firsthand is really good? So I taste. I taste a lot. I taste all the time. Of course, by the time we sit down to eat, it appears to everyone I am really staying on my diet. And I am then, because I've already eaten. Then, the food that is left over is too good to be thrown away, and I hate dabs of leftovers in the refrigerator, so it is up to me to take care of that problem too. Mother always said not to waste food, that there are people in the world starving to death. I never could see how MY eating could remedy the situation, but I felt duty-bound to do as she told me. Also, the expression "Clean your plate up" was used a lot in our home. I always did. I still do.

I will just mention briefly a word about exercise. It hurts. It's boring. It's a waste of time. I always take some form of nourishment with me when I walk. Peanut butter and crackers is a favorite, along with chocolate covered caramels. Why do I do this? Because I don't want to get caught away from home and get hungry.

Just recently I decided I would definitely go on a diet. I was going to count calories. I did really good at first. Then I began borrowing from the next meal. For example, if I was limited to 350 calories at noon, and went over that amount, I would simply promise to subtract it from the next meal's allotment. Then I would go over at that meal and promise to deduct from breakfast the next morning. At the present, I have borrowed calories from the next six months. While things are not going as I had intended, they are certainly going just as they usually do.

I think I will try more exercise next week. If I eat whatever I want, but exercise twice as much, I ought to get the same results. Makes sense to me. I think I will get one of those little baskets for my bike. You know, so I can take my lunch with me. You never know when I might get lost. You know how confused I get when I am away from home. Of course, I won't touch a bite of it unless I absolutely have to. Cross my heart!

Out of the Mouths of Babes

If I am not badly mistaken, I promised I was going to exercise twice as much and that I was going to do it by riding my bike twice as far as I usually do. I THINK I said "cross my heart." Wish I hadn't done that, because I really did not want to get on the bicycle.

But, a promise is a promise, so yesterday I put the old kick stand up and climbed aboard.

Things were going well for the first few blocks, then they took a turn for the worse (as things usually do for me).

Stopping so quickly I nearly went head over heels over the handlebar, I realized my pants leg was caught in the chain. Thankful that I had not fallen, I reached down to pull the fabric loose. Well, I pulled and I tugged, and I tugged and I pulled. Nothing, and I mean nothing, budged one little bit. I was caught tight.

You will have to get a mental picture of this in order to appreciate my situation. There I was, about four blocks from home, straddling my bike, trying to look as if nothing was wrong. Cars drove by and all the people waved.

I never saw so many friendly people in my life. The one time I wished no one was out but me, I quickly learned they were all out in their cars — and they were all driving right past the spot where I stood frozen.

I was thankful I had remembered to pack myself a little lunch, because I was sure I would still be in the same spot when the sun went down.

I couldn't put my right foot over the cross bar since it was the one caught. I tried putting the left leg over to the right side but that was impossible, too.

I couldn't lay the bike down unless I went down with it, and heaven only knows when I would have ever gotten up again. It seemed to me that one car kept driving by over and over again — I am sure wondering what I was doing standing in the same spot for over an hour.

Some little girl (bless her sweet heart) came and sat on the curb by me and asked all sorts of questions. "What are you doing, lady? Why don't you ride your bike, lady? Are you going to stay there all day, lady?" I told her I could hear her mother calling her, and she said her mother wasn't home, that she was staying with a baby sitter. She continued to sit and stare at me; I stared back at her. Normally I love children, but I was developing a real dislike for this little girl. I stuck my tongue out at her and she said, "That is not nice."

I replied that it was not nice to stare at people.

"I'm not staring. I just wonder if you are ever going to move."
Well, I will if I want to.
"Why don't you want to?"
Because I like it here.
"You aren't going to like it when that man gets home."
What man?
"The one that parks his big truck here."
He does not own the street.
"He thinks he does."

Beginning to feel desperate to get away from this little person, I discovered that by remaining astride the bike, with both feet on the ground I could inch myself forward by taking tiny, baby steps. It was really slow going, and looking back over my shoulder I could see the little girl following me every step of the way, saying over and over, "you sure do look funny, lady."

I suggested that she should go home, that the baby sitter probably was worried about her. She said "no," that she was the one who told her to stay outside and play. Well, I could understand why.

One car slowed down and asked if something was wrong. By now I was completely out of patience and I asked if everyone didn't ride their bike like I did.

The little picnic lunch I remembered I had in my basket was the only thing that kept me going, but the bad thing was I couldn't let go of the handlebars long enough to eat it.

But, "necessity is the mother of invention," as the saying goes, and I discovered I could lean forward and unwrap the sandwiches with my teeth and eat with no hands. I knew I might go down for the final count, but I would <u>not</u> go down hungry. The sun was beginning to set by the time I made it home. Cutting the pants leg loose with a pair of shears I had on the carport, I finally made it in the house.

That night I made an important decision . . . to sell my bike. A little girl was the only one to answer the ad, and she wanted to know where I lived. Said she knew a crazy lady that lived in her neighborhood that couldn't ride her bike, and she wanted to be sure that it wasn't me. It made me feel weak in the knees to think this child might show up on my doorstep. I thanked her for calling and said I had already sold it.

Weight a Minute —
The Fashion Industry Must Change

Someone is telling my weight and measurements all over the United States. I want it to stop! I want it to stop NOW! I resent it! A steady stream of specialty catalogs keep coming, one after another, from as far away as New York and California. "Big Mama," "More To Love," "Queen Sizes," etc. I would dearly love to receive some from Victoria's Secret. Does anyone think about that? They do not! Sure, maybe I couldn't order from them, but think how impressive it would be to have a few scattered around the living room. See? I just admitted it, I've been brain washed. We all have. We think "thin" is better. This MUST change. Now that I have gotten into this subject, I might as well tell you that the problem of attractive clothes for large women is a national disgrace that needs to be addressed. What better place to discuss problems than in this article?

Seriously, as I sat at home eating a piece of pecan pie with a cup of white chocolate cappuccino (I won't eat any supper), I realized we must take control of the fashion industry. I tell you ladies, I have had enough. No more hiding behind dressing room doors or racks for "plus" sizes. We must unite and take charge. The world is going to see a complete reversal of what is considered stylish.

First, we have to take over the modeling industry. We will not be able to use anyone who doesn't weight at least 160 pounds. Oh, I realize this is going to put a lot of girls out of work. Tough! Let them go home and eat to GAIN weight. Their goal in life will be to add pounds, not take them off. Just think. We will eliminate all the anorexia and bulimia we hear so much about. In other words, we will be actually saving lives. Possibly, we could receive the Nobel Prize. Even the textile business will thank us. It will take more fabric to make clothes. Talk about companies downsizing — they will be UP-sizing in more ways than one. Weight Watchers will have to change their program. Members will weigh in to see how much they have gained, rather than how much they have lost.

Doctors, you will have to get with the program too. Let's be honest. I know you mean well, but you really do put too much importance on weight. Has it helped? Oh, I admit some of us can lose weight. How many keep it off? Very, very few. We gain it back and some extra besides. It's a vicious cycle that causes a tremendous amount of tension. You tell us tension is a very bad thing, so we are going to eliminate much of that problem too. Doctors, I submit to you that skinny women everywhere have high blood pressure, heart problems, fallen arches, shingles, ingrown toenails, stiff joints and hemorrhoids. What do you blame their problems on? Do you tell them to go home and lose weight? Besides, WE heavier women last longer. WE are more durable.

I am so excited about this. I can see the headlines now. "Fat is Fun." "Plump is Pleasing." "Large is Lovely."

To prove my point, I took a poll recently of the local ministers. They all stated that it is what is inside a person that is important, not how much they weigh.

The infants at the daycare centers did not seem interested in obesity problems. They hardly even listened to the question.

The president of Lane Bryant Clothes said large women were definitely more attractive.

Even my mother always said good manners were the most important thing, and eating everything on your plate was the second most important.

I can see it now. The world IS GOING TO BE A BETTER PLACE. There won't be as much room left, but then we can't have everything.

Saving Money Can Be Expensive

Normally, I like to think of myself as a fairly level-headed person. Not prone to uncontrollable rages or hysterical behavior. However, there are certain things under certain conditions that can, and do, make me go off the deep end. Case in point: Scotch tape dispensers.

Each year after making it through the Christmas season and all the gift wrapping it involves, I always take a deep sigh of relief that I will not be faced again for awhile with boxes, ribbons, bows and Scotch tape. I know there are other brands, and I am not just picking on a particular name. They are all alike, they are all hateful, and none of them work after you pull off that first little piece.

Recently I purchased a wedding gift that had to be mailed out of town. I decided to let the store where I purchased it do the wrapping for me. Knowing I would be charged for the service, I was prepared to pay a reasonable amount. What I did not appreciate was the different levels of wrapping they offered. If I wanted to select the finest paper, the charge would be $4. With the largest and most attractive bow, it would be $1 more. It was at this point I reminded the lady I had purchased the gift from her store, and showed her the sales slip.

"It doesn't matter how much you paid for it, Ma'am. There is still a charge."

Oh, I thought maybe you thought I wanted to buy stock in the company.

"No, I just thought you wanted a first-class wrapping job."

So what else do you have this is not quite so first class?

"The next price range includes paper, our choice, not yours, and a much smaller bow."

How much smaller?

"Well, you can still see it."

What's next?

"The least expensive choice, if you don't care what it looks like anyway, is in a plain box with about three inches of ribbon taped somewhere on the top."

At this point I decided to buy what I needed and wrap it myself. Looking down my nose at the poor saleslady, I advised her just what I thought about the store charging their customers for gift wrapping. Why do we customers insist on taking our dissatisfaction out on sales people? It's another example of how unfair life can be.

I really don't have the time or space to go into detail about all that happened as I tried for three hours to get that small package wrapped. I will tell you I spent OVER $5 on paper, Scotch tape, ribbon and bows. Nothing went smoothly, but it was the Scotch tape that pushed me over the edge.

It was the tape that tore the paper, it was the tape that stuck to the bow and finally left it in shreds, and it was the tape that I could never find the end to every time I needed a new piece. How can anything on the face of this earth disappear so completely and so quickly as the end of Scotch tape? Never, and I repeat, NEVER, has it failed to happen. To date I have seven new rolls of Scotch tape that have no beginning or end. After about four hours of trying to wrap this gift myself, I returned to the store a very humble and contrite person and begged the same lady to please wrap it for me.

I no longer cared WHAT it cost. My sanity was at stake.

There's Nothing Like
A Very Special Friend

You show me an older person who lives alone, male or female, and I will show you a person who dreams of a special someone to share his or her life with. Age does not destroy the need for a companion to talk to, laugh with, or simply to enjoy things that are not special unless they can be shared.

A beautiful sunset, gently falling snow, the church choir blending their voices in a sacred hymn, the first sassy little spring flowers that peek their heads out of the soil, maybe even a rerun of "Mayberry."

Now, I know you are thinking, "Well, Edith Teasley has finally gone off the deep end." Not so! We all want someone who will look beyond the age factor (and the age spots) and understand that we still have the same feelings we had when we were young. I found that special person several years ago. I don't have him any more, and my life has not been the same since.

We met by accident, but we were attracted to each other immediately. Sure, I was a lot older and a lot taller, but that didn't interfere with our relationship. I'm sure others considered us an odd couple in the truest sense of the word. That didn't bother us either. We talked a lot, laughed a lot, and often just enjoyed being together. What others thought did not concern us in the least.

As our friendship grew, we often went riding. I have to admit his youth was responsible for a certain amount of recklessness on his part, and I would literally hold my breath when he would ride over the curb into someone's yard and then back to the street again. Knowing that it scared me, he would laugh and remind me he had never had a wreck.

One day he invited me to his home to see a special secret. Shucks, I trusted him completely and would have followed him anywhere. I met his family and knew immediately why he was so wonderful. The entire family was warm and gracious and made me feel welcome. I was so pleased to know they had no objection to the age difference.

Leading me into the den, he proudly showed me "Snicker" and her babies. Then, with wisdom far beyond his years he asked me if I knew why she didn't have more. Looking extremely serious he explained it was because she didn't have any more in her.

Can you understand how wonderful it was to know this special, handsome, tow-headed 5-year-old young man would watch for me to come by his house, so we could ride together?

Later, after being out of town for several months, I came home to discover his little bicycle was no longer propped up in his garage. The house was vacant, and a for sale sign with "SOLD" across it was in the yard.

Well, I still ride my bike, but it isn't the same any more. I never go by his house that I don't think of him.

I really loved him, and I really enjoyed being with him.

I really, really miss him.

Mrs. Doolittle I Am Not

One thing I really enjoy is the family of squirrels that eat at my feeders regularly. I can see them as I sit at my window typing. There must be at least twenty-five that take turns eating. I love seeing them holding a kernel of corn in their tiny little paws eating in their own dainty manner.

I have two feeders now, so that means twice as much corn and twice the expense, but, gosh, I don't mind. They have given me so much pleasure, that anything I can do to make them happy and to insure that they continue to feel welcome in my yard . . . well, I'm happy to do it.

I say I don't mind the expense but that is not completely true because there are other things I could spend that money on, but when the little darlings find the feeders empty they seem to get a little upset. In fact, they have learned to climb on the back of the deacon's bench on my front porch and look in my front window. I wouldn't mind that if they just didn't look so angry. I keep the drapes closed now because, to tell you the truth, I resent being the object of their unrelenting stares. Silly of me because I'm sure they would never harm me.

I have a close neighbor who loves the birds the way I love my squirrels. She feeds them regularly, or at least she would if MY critters would quit stealing the birdseed.

I was not aware there was a problem until I walked over for a visit one afternoon. Noticing some contraption on the birdhouse pole, I asked what on earth the thing was. It looked to me like a dishpan turned upside down. Well, it was as if the floodgates had been opened and all her problems with my squirrels came rushing out. She explained it was her latest effort to thwart their never ending attempts to get the birdseed. She went on to explain it had worked, but now the squirrels had learned to jump from a branch of her magnolia tree to the top of the birdhouse. One had actually managed to get inside and sat there grinning at her as he ate. Furthermore, when she tried to chase him away with a broom, the impudent thing BARKED at her. Right! Like I believe a squirrel can bark. She went on to suggest that if I would quit feeding them, that with a little luck they would all go away. I, in turn, suggested she quit feeding the birds and maybe THEY would go away.

Knowing I had planted one tomato plant and a bed of Periwinkles, she warned me the squirrels would eat every single thing I was trying to grow.

Feeling she was just a little hurt over the situation, I ignored her warnings but decided just to be on the safe side I would put out even more corn, to keep them satisfied.

The next morning I looked outside just in time to see one of my little animal friends running across the lawn with a tiny green tomato in his grubby paws, and then discovered he had stripped the Periwinkles of every single bloom.

I grabbed my broom and dashed outside to chase the ugly thing away, and it actually turned around and barked at me. Can you believe that? As good as I have been to those ungrateful, nasty creatures.

Well, I assure you of one thing. My neighbor and I are closer than ever because we share a common goal. To rid the neighborhood of these despicable, thieving, hateful pests.

Mission Impossible Runs Out Of Gas

Do you think I never go anywhere? Not so! Do you think other people are the only ones who take wonderful vacations? Not so!

I am tired of hearing all about cruises, trips overseas, and long visits to Disneyland. I am not a dull person; I go places too. I just try not to brag about my own exciting experiences. As a matter of fact, my daughter and I are planning a very special trip to Columbus — not Ohio — Columbus, Mississippi. Why should we go hundreds of miles when we have our very own vacation haven only thirty minutes away?

We usually take a trip every summer, but we have learned to plan carefully. Many vacations end in disaster because of lack of planning. This year we decided that she will be in charge of the route we take and the van. I will be in charge of where we eat and the things we will see. (Incidentally, she asked me when had she ever given me permission to use her name in my articles. She went on to say that is the sort of thing that makes lawyers wealthy.) As you can see, she can be a little "testy" about our relationship, so I do try not to irritate her any more than necessary.

Finally our plans were complete and last week we were excited as we rolled down the driveway and headed for Columbus. Friends were lined up to wish us a safe journey. Sakes alive! That is not true. Guess I get carried away sometimes trying to make stories more enjoyable. The truth of the matter was no one saw us leave except the neighbor's cat that sleeps on top of my car, and he was mad because I made him move. Then there was the one squirrel I can't run off, and he gave us a bored look over his shoulder as we drove away.

We gave serious consideration to stopping for the night in order to break the trip, but since we got such an early start, we decided to drive straight through.

About two miles out on the bypass, the van began to sputter and then slowly rolled to a complete stop. There is something about an old woman standing helplessly by her car that makes men drive right on by without so much as a glance, but you put a young attractive woman on the highway by a stalled car and men will slam on their brakes, come to a screeching halt, and beg to be allowed to help. Guess who I suggested stand by the van?

The problem was that we were out of gas. Some time later one of the young men that had stopped to help, drove back with enough gas to get us to Columbus. By then, we were hot, tired, and hungry and just a little of the excitement had begun to wear off. In spite of this, we were still being civil to each other and were determined to have fun.

In an effort to lighten the mood, I suggested we eat at Woody's. Woody's is a wonderful place to eat, but it is a very dark place to eat. Since my eyesight is not what it once was, (actually, nothing is what it once was), I picked up the little decorative lamp to read the menu. I saw my companion roll her eyes — always an indication that I have done some little thing to irritate her. When I attempted to give my order to another customer, she clinched her fists — another bad sign.

Pretending not to notice, I remarked that they were featuring ostrich and I wanted to order a drumstick. Do you know how long the leg of an ostrich is? Can you imagine the size of a drumstick? I thought it was hilarious. She turned white, stood up, and said through her clinched teeth, "We are going home now."

Talk about a cold shoulder — we didn't even need the air conditioner on the way home.

Trying to make light of the situation, I remarked that if "you know who" had gotten her "you know what" busy with her responsibilities, we would not have run out of gas. That was what had spoiled the trip, not me. She very slowly and deliberately pulled off and stopped on the side of the road, turned to look at me, and said sweetly, "Mother, I am not only your best friend, I am probably your only friend — so watch it." I'm watching it.

To Err Is Human
(and dangerous)

One of my grandchildren was having a really difficult time in school. Knowing there was no problem in the "brains" department, her mother began searching for some answers to the problem. Was she just not paying attention? Was she not challenged enough? Did the teacher not explain things clearly enough? Was she not well? As usual, the entire family began to be concerned. This little girl was exceptionally bright, yet her grades seemed to be falling each week. There had to be an answer.

It occurred to her mother that often the child did not respond as quickly as she should when spoken to. Could her hearing be bad? An appointment was made with the doctor, but he too, was puzzled over the situation and suggested a specialist in Memphis, Tennessee. Now, I don't need to tell you mothers that nothing is too good for our children. Therefore my daughter took off from work, asked me to ride with them, and the appointment was made.

By now, my granddaughter had caught on to the fact that we were all very concerned, and she began to look sad, and depressed over the prospect of having a disability. Knowing how cruel other children can be, we dreaded knowing that she would be considered "different." To make up for the emotional hurt we knew she would suffer, we tried to compensate by planning special treats while in Memphis. No one, including the teacher, pressured her to bring her grades up, knowing for the first time that she was already doing the best she could under the circumstances.

Her mother cried one day as she admitted she had grounded the child once for failing to bring homework home. How could she, when she couldn't hear what the teacher said? No, she didn't ask her to repeat it, because she was afraid the other children would laugh at her. This simply broke our hearts, so her parents decided to hire a private tutor to get her caught up. My granddaughter smiled so bravely and said that would be fine with her. She was so precious about the whole thing . . . never complained, just seemed resigned to her fate.

We decided to give her something to look forward to, so reservations were made at the finest motel, a trip to the zoo, and even Libertyland.

Getting up early the day of the appointment, we headed for Memphis. My granddaughter sat between us uncomplaining and adorable. I did notice that she had no problem hearing us in the car, and then realized it was because she was sitting so close and looking right at us when we spoke. The thought crossed my mind that she would have no problem learning to lip read.

When the doctor came in he spoke directly to Stephanie, and she said, "How do you do," as she had been taught to do. Her manners were impeccable and we were so proud of her.

Her mother began to tell the doctor the details of why we were there, and as she described the situation at school, her eyes filled with tears. The doctor smiled kindly and said for her not to worry, things were probably not as bad as she thought. I mentioned how puzzled I was that she seemed to be able to hear in the car, and asked if he could explain that. Smiling again, he said he wanted to examine her and run some tests before he came to any conclusion. It seemed to me he was smiling a lot, under the circumstances.

We were left to wait, and wait, and wait. Finally Stephanie returned to the room and I could sense some fear in her that had not been there before. I pulled her up in my lap and began reminding her of the fun we were going to have after the doctor was through. She interrupted me in the middle of a sentence and asked her mother, "Are you going to be mad if he says I can hear?" The doctor returned (still smiling) and said he had good news and bad news. The good news was she could probably hear better than we could, and the bad news was she had been able to fool everyone.

Well! The temperature in that room dropped at least forty degrees. Taking Stephanie by the arm, my daughter marched out of that hospital with her daughter's feet never touching the ground. Actually, at this point, I feared for Stephanie's life, and felt it wasn't worth a plugged nickel. Reaching the car I pushed my way in so I was positioned in the middle. I knew she had done a very bad thing, but I didn't think she needed to die for it.

No words were spoken as we headed home. No nice motel, no zoo, no Libertyland . . . no nothing. Just silence for a solid three and a half hours.

I don't know what transpired between the two of them after they reached home; I do know none of us saw much of Stephanie for about two months. Every time I asked about her, it seemed she was catching up on homework.

Really Burned Up

Knowing that football season is here again, (I know this to be a fact, since it took me forty-five minutes to drive from Longmeadow subdivision to Kroger), I know I should lock all my doors, close the blinds, and tack a note on my door that says I will be gone for several months. (Desperate times call for desperate measures.) I don't want my daughter to invite me to another game.

Our relationship depends on it. I love her very, very much — I would do anything in my power for her — I think she is intelligent, witty, beautiful, good company, and my best friend, but, I will not go to another football game with her.

Last year, I did agree to go to an afternoon game. I do irrational things on a regular basis, but that was a really bad decision on my part. What I don't understand is why she thought she needed me. It isn't as though she was going to be the only one there. Thousands of fans occupied the bleachers.

The idea that I would be any company was inconceivable if not downright ludicrous. I am not good company at any time, certainly not at a football game. I don't understand one single thing about it, except that I really love to hear the band play and I get excited when I know the Mississippi State Bulldogs are winning. Beyond that, I am completely lost.

My daughter always enticed me with promises of special little treats — cookies, chips, candy and drinks. She would take along a cushion for me to sit on, a cute little Bulldog cap, pom-poms for me to wave, and a cow bell to ring. It didn't take long for the pom-poms and the cow bell to disappear because she said I was only supposed to use them when our side was winning. How was I to know that when I never could tell who had the ball? Anyway, that left me with just food to pass the time. If you know me at all, you know food is the last thing I need.

In a moment of weakness last year, I agreed to go with her to an afternoon game. It was a little warm, but a beautiful day when we reached the stadium, and I quickly settled in with food in each hand and a cold drink by my side. As the game progressed, so did the sun until it was shining on the right side of my face and neck at close to 110 degrees. I mentioned to my "best friend" that I was getting pretty warm. She patted me on the arm like I was a small child and assured me that I was just fine.

I tried turning in different positions and finally turned completely around, facing the people behind me. This seemed to make them uneasy and my daughter said I was embarrassing her, so I had no other option except to grow more and more uncomfortable. I was hotter than I had ever been in my life, and by the third quarter, I remarked I was afraid that I was going to burn. She said not to worry, that I was barely getting pink. By the time that game was over, even my eyelashes hurt.

Driving home, she remarked that maybe it would be a good idea to use a little lotion on my face and neck before going to bed. To bed? Who could go to bed? I was hurting just standing in the middle of the floor. The thought of lying down with anything touching my skin made me long for death.

That evening, I went from one store to another accumulating every sunburn remedy on the market. Nothing helped. It took a good five days before the blisters began to peel. I couldn't turn my head, look up, or look down. Any movement at all from my shoulders up was agony. I was burned to a crisp and thought at one point that my head would simply shrivel up and drop off. Not mine — it stayed right where it was intended to stay, as a constant reminder that I must never ever, under any circumstances, go to another afternoon game. In fact now that I think about it, my daughter has never invited me again.

How lucky can a person be?

About the Author

Edith Teasley first began writing for the First Baptist Church News Letter. Noticed by the local paper, she has since been published weekly in the Life Style section of the Starkville Daily News. It was because of the response and encouragement from readers, family, and friends that she has decided to have a collection of her stories published in book form.

Since her family is close knit and fun loving, (and because they can turn any event into a comedy of errors) she is able to get her material from actual experiences. Edith admits she is grateful they all have a sense of humor or she would have been disowned by now.

Originally from Memphis, Tennessee, she has lived many years in Starkville, Mississippi, and confesses she loves the slower pace of a small town.

She is the mother of four daughters, nine granddaughters, three great granddaughters and one great grandson.

Retired, she stays busy with her "stories", does some oil painting when time permits, is an avid reader, and has performed with the Starkville Community Theater. She states she is having the time of her life as a senior citizen.